M-Clave Beginnings

THE RISE OF A NEW HERO

REY CENA

Contents

EZ
Door
&
Credit
VICTORY
PART
&
Credit

Have you noticed how music sometimes makes you feel stronger, lightweight, flexible and free? Music is capable of this and much more.

I. EZ DOOR

Sunlight was lost over the skyline of the city of Los Angeles. The evening lights gave way to the tapestry of stars that illuminated the night sky contrasting with bars and shops. Chinatown began to come alive with bright lights framed like a beautiful postcard. Advertisements bombarded posters and various images on the dark blue background gradually became a distant and unattainable black velvet. The majestic palm trees moved slowly with the wind of a warm summer evening in a city full of glamour where the picturesque traces left outside those living on the streets, camouflaged by indifference.

A van headed from Plaza Mariachi along the road to Sunset Boulevard's moderate traffic. From the sky, the streets resembled the Milky Way, with a long path illuminated on a black carpet. The lights of the houses and buildings were like bright, tiny stars. Every being a world, and each world a huge human encyclopedia.

The vehicle passed in front of Wings, one of the famous local live band stages, which was beginning to fill with people. They were close, only a few blocks away from their destination.

Stage Chord, with its majestic look, started presenting a vertical neon sign that anticipated the bands playing that night. There had been famous bands that played there.

The place was built about fifty years ago and remodeled with the arrival of the eighties, extending to its two premises located next door. Graffiti occupied the entire corner extending half a block to the entrance

STAGE CORD
SPIRITUAL REFUGE
EZ DOOR

and a large gate guarded by two Hulky security guards wearing leather clothes. Seen from above, it was like a diamond and the sublime decor gave the place a real gem look. The bar, full of neon lights, reflected on the bottles and a mirror eight meters long, penetrating amplified laser lights. The speakers sounded loud with excellent clarity. The triangle formed in the corner. The stage was located about fifteen meters long, on a grand stage where instruments, the lights, and smoke were the main stars. A huge curved screen behind the drum kit displayed multimedia content projected as the bands played and dark velvet curtains added an air of mystery to the stage.

A huge number of people were clustered inside Stage Chord, eagerly waiting to watch the bands that were performing that night, taking advantage of drink specials and many more were still waiting to get in. The tables were occupied and placed to the sides to make way for all who entered.

The van stopped a few meters from the door. It was painted black with drawings of green and orange that seemed to float in the air. The blue lights under the fenders gave it an outer space look. EZ Door had arrived. The driver got off and gave two pats to the side of the vehicle and opened the side door. Inside were three musicians and their equipment.

The driver took the opportunity to light a cigar while the band was getting down from the van. When the last of the members came down he took a long puff and went to one of them.

"Carlos, do you want us to bring down the equipment? It would be best to park the van around the corner."

"Yeah, just give me a second," he indicated as his gaze turned to a girl who was a few meters from them who waved at him.

She wore a black skirt and a red jacket that matched the color of her lips and a white complexion. She wore loose, slightly wavy blond hair and her face perfectly carved with fine features, highlighted the twinkle in her blue eyes were a sufficiently provocative invitation for him to run toward her. They hugged and kissed passionately while the driver watched the scene and extinguished the cigarette on the floor.

"Today will be a great night, look at all these people!" she said as she held his hand and watched the line of people waiting to get in.

"You're the only audience I want," he said. While kissing her hand he whispered, "We must bring the instruments backstage. You're on the list, see you inside." He turned and headed for the van.

The other band members were bringing down the bass amp. Carlos took the two boxes with John's instruments and the drums and the drum plates. They entered through a door with a ramp away from the front door where an unexpected tall, muscular man introduced himself as one of the security guards. After verifying their identities, he allowed them to come in by opening up the door. They walked down a hallway with painted bricks and finally reached the dressing room located behind the stage. It was a room where band members were able to relax. That night they had Spiritual Refuge and then, EZ Door performing. Upon entering, they accommodated their instruments. Carlos pulled out his guitar and then played some arpeggios to warm-up his fingers. With all the adrenaline he just wanted to go out and play.

Carlos was looking for John, but the bassist said he had gone to park the van. John was an old friend of Carlos, about eight years older and was characterized as one of those friends who were in the good, the bad and the very bad. John was the older brother he always wished to have. He could go to him when he could not find the self-confidence he needed and when he needed advice that parents and younger siblings could not give. Especially, because John took care of Carlos as he did to his younger siblings Kimberly and Christopher, but no blood ties existed between them. In addition, if it had not been for John, he would have not met Cindy.

EZ Door came playing for almost a year, but that night was great, it was a presentation at the Stage Chord, the same scenario that saw the posters of their favorite bands, that place of myth and legend that had grown from a dream to a real experience. They had rehearsed throughout the month, balancing time with the university and family obligations. Carlos' parents had divided opinions about it. Her mother disagreed but accepted it, unlike his father, supporting him and had given the approval to go ahead.

Bassist Ethan wore a black shirt with the logo of his favorite band, Theludge. Drummer Roy seemed the quietest of the three but was someone else when he began playing the pads of the new drums. Carlos wore a yellow silk shirt with small black spots, a leather jacket and black pants. His appearance gave him a fresh and impressive frontman of the band. One of his virtues is his charisma on stage and people took notice. They had managed to make some good shows getting a small group of followers who enjoyed their music.

The Spiritual Refuge was sounding very tight. The musicians were silently listening to the theme, "Power Within" where the drums and bass resounded contrasting with hypnotic guitars sounds. The voice was melodic, and everything seemed to be embedded like puzzle pieces. Ethan looked at Carlos shaking his head.

"What a sound!" Ethan said, making a sweep over his bass.

"Did you listen to the people? must be over 1,000 people out there. I want to go up now!" articulated Roy as he punched in the air as if in front of his drums.

"Yes, they are!" Carlos said, raising his right hand to silence his friends. "Listen to that voice, Dave knows how to make things sound good after all," referring to the lead singer of another band.

"They have played the same songs for two years," Roy said as he blew imaginary two disks "If you do not sound good after so long, you should get new material or be forgotten. Dust to dust."

"When we come out, we will be amazing, plus we sound better than they did," Ethan said calmly.

"This is our night," Roy said with excitement.

"Of course! We are at the Stage Chord!" Carlos shouted as he stood and crashed his palm with the musicians.

There was a knock on the door of the dressing room to let them know it was time to load their equipment and instruments to the stage. They began to move the equipment up the ramp leading to the stage. They bumped with the other musicians greeting and congratulating them by the stellar performance. Roy waved as Carlos saluted Dave, like a silent movie.

John entered the stage carrying water bottles and arranged towels and some picks.

"Five-minutes," he told them as they checked their equipment.

"Hey, thanks again brother," said Carlos as he checked his guitar belt.

"Nothing to thank me for," he winked and popped open a beer bottle. "Just remember that someday I want to see you guys at Wings."

The curtain opened and the band started to a pure frenzy with guitar melodies which was blending with the bass and drums. The lights fell on Carlos clothes and felt the power of music invading his whole body, every chord emphasized his smile when singing, while Ethan was moving around the stage. The stage lit up with red and green lights, colors highlighted the musicians and the audience was very connected to the band. Cindy jumped and sang the themes in the front row alongside the fence. There was so much adrenaline that Carlos had failed to see it the first time and was so attuned to the music that just before presenting the second song he looked around and people felt the energy in the room. At that time the guitars and the drums marked one of the hits of the band. Drums shocks spread across the room and voices filled every corner with their melodies. They were at their best and the audience took notice. Several musicians of Spiritual Refuge were watching the band from the side of the stage and applauded each of the songs as if they were part of the public.

Their set came to an end. The show concluded the evening with gratitude and the promise of seeing them on their next tour date.

When the curtain closed, they hugged and congratulated each other. They were still just meters from the ground, so much adrenaline and excitement. John came to greet them.

"Congratulations guys! You did an amazing show," he smiled and helped disassemble the drums.

"This was amazing, even Dave was watching us," said Carlos.

"Yes, they were really amazed," replied John.

"Yes, because we are EZ Door," Ethan said as fist bumped in the air.

"Hey, they are also good. Keep those comments to the van. I do not want to end up fighting again, okay?" said Carlos as he put away his guitar while John watched with approval to his comment.

They brought the instruments backstage; they were greeted with some of the Spiritual Refuge and then they all went to the floor to have a few drinks. When passing through the floor people congratulated them and really made them feel like rock stars.

Carlos asked John to let him know when they were ready to carry their instruments so that he can go grab a drink with Cindy.

"Go ahead, I'll go to chat with some fans, I will tell them I'm your

EZ
DOOR
THELUDGE

rep. I also have the right to have fun," John said in anticipation as reading the mind of Carlos who was speechless and only managed to say, "Ok."

At the side of the hall was an empty table. Cindy hurried to sit while Carlos went to get some drinks at the bar. He had ordered a margarita for her and him a drink that reminded his Latin roots he loved because it mixed the taste of mezcal with lemon juice and cocoa.

After greeting several fans who intercepted them, he got to his destination, bringing their drinks to the table and sat as if he had been standing for hours. They drank and drank as they looked into their eyes. He felt that fatigue disappeared as they gazed into each other's eyes. They had met at a restaurant. John was with him that day to find an amplifier for his guitar and stopped for gas. It was about noon, so they entered a restaurant to eat something to continue the journey. Cindy worked there as a waitress and when Carlos saw her, and felt he had connected with her instantly. It was as if he had known her for years. But he was lacking courage to approach her. She got close to take the order. He could barely articulate his order because he was fascinated watching her eyes, but he lowered his eyes when she looked at him. John caught on quickly and asked the same order for both. She left with a smile leaving them alone. A romantic song was playing in the background that was a hit at that time. A song titled, "If You Are Gone" by Rey Cena.

"What's wrong brother? That girl broke you up like a puzzle, are you in love?"

"…I think so." as he lifted his eyes slowly and looked into the distance. "Those eyes, that smile, it never happened to me before."

"That's good my brother, then ask her out already," said John, as he laughed and threw himself back on his chair.

"Oh sure, everything is so easy, you know how bad I was with women recently. I will not suffer again."

"…the one who risks…"

"Already! I need to concentrate on the band. It's the only thing that makes me feel good," he said, directing his gaze to the window.

John got up and told him he had to go to the bathroom. Within minutes, she appeared to take their orders and capturing his attention on an exchange of glances she asked,

"Is it true that you play in a band? It is the first time we got a visit from a famous musician." The comment made him drop his eyes as he shyly looked down.

"Well, it's not that we are famous for the moment..." he said correcting himself not to sound insecure. "I say, yes, we are playing and play well, indeed, soon we will play on the stage of Wings and from then on no one will stop us." As she watched him with interest, her face looked like a tomato because she knew he was exaggerating.

"How awesome! I would like to see you play," she said with a smile, as he saw John from far made a sign of approval and he understood he had something to do with it.

That was the beginning a year ago and now they were there, at the Stage Chord, it was a dream materialized.

"You know, I'm so happy that we are sharing this moment, I feel like I could look down and see clouds at my feet."

"I am also very happy," she said, leaving her drink on the table to get closer to kiss him.

Ethan and Roy were nearby, captivated by the music and the group of girls beside them on the dance floor. The DJ was playing hit after hit and people seemed mesmerized as the place vibrated.

A few hours later, the musicians were packing up their equipment to the van while the girls were getting in. It was time to leave.

"What happened, grandpa? You coming back home alone tonight?" Roy slurred with obvious intoxication.

"I think you're the one going home alone my friend," John responded.

"Roy... quiet, get your stuff and do not bother him me," Carlos directed Roy toward the van.

"You know how he gets," Carlos said to John.

"Yeah, I know. It's okay though. Tomorrow I need to get up early to help my sister with some paperwork."

"Ok, come on then. And thanks again brother. If it wasn't for you..."

"Ahh...shut up!" John gave Carlos a hug before climbing into the van.

The van started, Carlos was looking for directions from the G.P.S to take the girls home, and then leave the equipment in the garage where Ethan lives.

John stopped at the red light and took a glimpse on the street at one of the posters that promoted bands that month. Despite the dim lights, the black letters on green background from the posters could be seen clearly. He was filled with pride to see the name of EZ Door showing the date of that night which had been a success. It was the start of something big, he could feel it, but his thoughts were interrupted when the lights changed and had to start driving again.

Night contrasted with the solitude of the streets as the headlights were making their way to their destinations. After a long journey, they were about to turn a corner to return to get on to the 101 freeway, and it was then when John saw about thirty meters away a car with one of its rear doors open. Inside the van Roy was sleeping while Ethan was highly entertained with the girl whom he was with. Carlos was attentive to John's comments and moved forward to see what was happening while Cindy looked without understanding what was going on.

At ten meters, John saw what appeared to be two or three people and thought someone had a broken-down car and were helping him, but when they were close enough saw a man grappled with what appeared as a homeless person trying to get him into the car. John hit the brakes of the van and alerted his friends. Without hesitation John got out while Carlos shouted at Ethan that John had gone down and that they should go with him to help.

"Cindy, call 911!" shouted Carlos.

The street was lit by one of the lanterns and lights of the van seemed to enlarge the figure of the attacker.

John approached the men and yelled. "Hey! What happened friend?" addressing the homeless man.

But the man sobbed and could barely speak. As John approached, he realized the man's mouth was dripping with blood. The rest of the man's face was obscured by a hoodie, but John assumed the rest of him was in a similar state.

"Leave him alone!" John started yelling.

"Mind your own business," the stranger said, giving another swift kick to the homeless man on the floor.

He had his face covered and could not be seen more than the eyes.

"Let him go. We've called the police," Carlos screamed, but the man approached with the intention to work things out differently.

Carlos ran to John and stood behind him. Ethan was coming down from the van and Roy was still asleep. The girls were cuddled calling the police.

The homeless man screamed in pain as he struggled with the attacker who tried to lift him off the ground to take to the car.

The driver got off and began to approach quietly without being noticed wearing a dark mask. John felt the danger and even more when he saw Carlos behind him who shouted to go look for help.

John launched toward the man coming close to him and began to fight while turning a deaf-ear to Carlos who ran to push the attacker who was with the homeless man. Both fell to the ground and the homeless man began crawling along the sidewalk. Carlos kicked the man away as he watched John fall to the ground after the blows from the driver.

In the distance, he spotted Ethan starting to approach with Roy, who did not understand what was happening; they were still far away.

Everything happened so fast he did not notice when John was laid to the ground and as he tried to sit up, he felt the first gun shot.

It seemed that time had stopped, and Carlos began screaming, and screaming like never before in his life. The other attacker kicked Carlos from behind and grabbed him as Carlos looked at the driver who had a distorted smile by the mask. The shot had hit him in the stomach, forcing John to fall on his knees as he crouched in pain.

Carlos hit with his elbows the kidnapper who was grabbing him and saw the driver give John three stab wounds to his friend as he was reciting something that was interpreted as *"... I caught your soul, your spirit ... it belongs to me now ..."* while holding a medal that was around his neck. John dropped down like a mannequin.

The man was smiling while the other man knocked Carlos unconscious as he listened to the cries of his friends mixed with the siren of the police patrols and everything faded, until complete darkness fell upon him.

II. LAU

Moving slowly and not realizing where Carlos was, everything seemed messy and out of place. With every step, his legs felt like he was in an ocean of gelatin and despite trying to raise his arms to touch his head, felt sore, as if he was carrying something heavy. The lights seemed shrouded in fog—discolored. He felt the need to run, but at every step seemed to sink deeper into quicksand. His body shaking, sweating, restless and trapped in a dream which he could not wake up, fought in vain against a force that kept him prisoner, smothering his mind.

He heard barking surrounding him, and then a hollow sound and when looking at the floor the image of a dog lying sideways, bleeding, moving his legs as if running continuously unable to do so, within a kaleidoscope. The image changed and saw a silhouette behind him. He wanted to scream, but there was no word that could come out of his mouth. The image of John disjointed and the sound of the shot echoed even in his ears. Everything was unreal, yet vivid once more. A silhouette approached the body of his friend trapping his soul with evil eyes, watching him with frivolous indifference of a dead look. Suddenly, he was on a deserted street. The light of the sidewalk began to flash on and off. In front of him, John's silhouette stretched out his hands and started moving his mouth. The sound was very consistent, but it was not necessary to hear him because he could read his lips something along the lines of *"help me."*

Carlos woke up shaken with tears in his eyes. Surrounded by the darkness of his room looking at the clock and he saw the time marked 3:00 am. He laid there, staring at the ceiling of his room, thinking. The nightmares were recurring every two weeks and sometimes more often. It has been more than a year since John had been killed. His thoughts were spinning trying to turn back time, formulating that moment hundreds of variables looking even in dreams to change the course of events. He could not take his mind off how everything turned out to be.

The police did not find the murderers, nor the vehicle involved despite all the details that had been given to them. There were also no traces of the homeless man who was attacked. It was as if the earth had swallowed him. He closed his eyes…he still had a few hours to rest.

...

There was a knock on the door which woke him up. The clock showed 7:15 am. He dressed quickly and went to the dining room where his family was organizing breakfast.

"Buenos días, hijo," said a female in Spanish, as the young man came up to kiss her.

"Buenos días, mamá," he replied.

"Do me a favor and call your brother and sister. I am finishing cooking the bacon."

Araceli, a stylized black-haired woman with strong Latin features placed ham on the pan and took coffee to the table where a Caucasian corpulent man was putting on a tie while sitting at the table. He looked at the young man and greeted him with a smile.

"How are you son? Araceli reached over and dropped two slabs of thick, crispy bacon on his plate.

Is today when you have the exam at school?"

"Good day, dad. No, the exam is next week. I finished work late last night," he said as he headed into the corridor to look for his brother and sister.

Robert, his father, talked out loud as if there was an audience who would listen.

"Today it will be a difficult Friday because of all those cars on the street, it's crazy. I hope this spring festival brings me at least good customers." Coffee was served while capturing the look of Araceli and pointed his head toward the TV.

The television showed fairly busy traffic near *Plaza Latina*. The spring carnival first began to show its colors. For three days, the entire Hispanic culture would be the epicenter of a unique event where a lot of arts would be developed around a wide variety of entertainment. Many tourists came to enjoy the colorful city, food, and especially, the artists with their great performances.

Carlos bumped into Kimberly, his younger sister who was leaving the bathroom. She was wearing a yellow shirt and pink tights. Her hair was curly, and her features were a carbon copy of Araceli. The mark of the pillow on her face showed that she was not yet fully awake. Despite having sixteen years old Carlos still saw her as his baby sister. Hugged and touched her head shaking slightly with intent to wake her up.

Christopher left his room hastily adjusting his shoes bumping into them. The boy smiled showing his braces and glasses. His body was similar to that of Robert, short and blondish hair, somewhat overweight for nine years old. Carlos was a perfect mix between his parents, and that mixed of his Latin roots and the stylized body of his mother, with height and Caucasian traits of his father.

"Chris!" shouted Carlos. "I'll grab the you child!" Carlos started moving his arms like a huge robot that was about to catch him.

From the dining room, they heard the voice of Araceli who called for breakfast. The news was showing the extended weather forecast announcing sunny and warm for the weekend.

When they sat down, Robert commented that this weekend could be the opportunity to go for a walk to the festivities.

"As long as you do not stay up late on Saturday selling cars," Araceli stated while handing the plate with eggs to Carlos.

"I hope that today we get a lot of good sales. You know how hard it is when a customer comes in and makes you waste time," looking like a statue.

"Look, last week a couple came to the dealership and the girl was the one who seemed to want to buy a car. We go by a list, so when it's your turn, you go to the client that came in."

"And then you go to the end of the list." Araceli said knowing the story.

"It's all a matter of luck," whispered Carlos to his brother and he could not help laughing as she took the coffee pot. His comment went unnoticed as Robert nodded and responded to Araceli.

"Exactly! And you know that the girl came with a notebook and said very loosely while her boyfriend walked between the cars like a dove… 'we were looking at several dealerships and test drove six cars but we cannot decide, so I'm here to try four more but I will not buy anything until next year' " said Robert doing the woman's voice, "and you know what? they were writing down all the characteristics of all those cars!".

"For a moment, I thought I was in one of those hidden cameras showing on television. I was worried that I was going to come out too fat!".

Christopher and Kimberly laughed as Carlos joined in except for Araceli who looked puzzled.

"So, what did you do honey?" Araceli asked.

"Because I saw her so confused, and her boyfriend seemed not to care, so I said 'all these cars are very similar in size and equipment, tell me what you are looking for because apparently you have not found anything' and she looked at her notes while I noticed other customers coming in and Joe who is one of the oldest at the dealership looked at me pointing and making fun of me."

"It would be difficult for me to choose a car," Kimberly whispered shyly to Carlos.

"I wanted to send these two to Joe, so I applied what we learned in the sales course and I asked her 'the four cars you want to try at our dealership, are they the same as those you tried at the other dealerships? tell me something, in the sense of space and comfort, were the cars similar?' and saw that her face became thoughtful and she said 'mmm … the truth is you are right' and then I gave my final opinion 'well then, there is no need to drive these cars' and her face changed with anger and confusion then asked me to go to the restroom, and that's when I left them alone and when she came out grabbed her boyfriend who looked like an adornment and left."

"Well done, dear!" Araceli said, with conviction as she stroked her husband's face and got up to take the empty plates.

"Some people do not understand that we are car salesmen and if they are not serious to buy we lose the opportunity to sell to someone who is. Then the next clients that came in bought from Joe. If I had not touched that couple, I would have made a sale! I will get even with Joe," replied Robert in a convincing manner.

"You really know how to deal with customers, dad!" Christopher said, with his grin face as he stacked bacon and eggs over several rolls.

"You know child you have to have character!" he said, and smiled back with a wink.

Carlos then joined in finishing his coffee and put on his sweatshirt preparing to leave.

"I'll be back later today. I will go with Cindy to the Help Center. We have some things to donate."

"You coming back for dinner?" Araceli asked as she passed the coffee pot to her husband.

"No, I want to take Cindy to see that superhero movie. I could use that to clear my head a little, I had not been sleeping well these last few weeks."

Robert looked up crossing eyesight with his wife and looking at Carlos he said, "Take my car. Today I will be back early to watch the game, sports will be tonight's family night."

"Yes!" yelled Christopher, who enjoyed watching the games with his father.

"And it will be dance night for the girls, we can use that dancing and singing game," Araceli said, looking at her daughter.

Kimberly answered her affirmatively nodding with a smile.

"Thanks, dad," Carlos said, as he grabbed his backpack and headed for the door.

"Call me if you need anything. Don't send me messages," responded Robert.

After some recommendations from his father to avoid traffic, he left. Robert finished eating his breakfast while Kimberly and Christopher got ready to go to school.

John's loss was also a blow not only to Carlos, but also for his family. Robert was very fond of him because he knew John's family. He was a great friend of his father and despite the age difference between John and his son always saw them as Robert's kids. The day of the tragedy him and his wife overcame what happened by supporting each other. The strength and unity were able to overcome grief, although losing someone is something you can never recover from. They were a young couple who just passed their 40s, there were still many battles to fight. Robert supported his son with his band, although Araceli prioritized his studies.

After John's death, Carlos started having nightmares. He kept them hidden from his family. He felt guilty and anxious, however he had to be strong for his siblings as he was with Cindy. Robert talked with Araceli about how lucky they were not having lost Carlos. Despite being the eldest son, they had put so much attention that at times they realized they were losing control over their other two children. Kimberly was very shy, and they noticed it, so they constantly motivated her. Christopher also faced problems of bullying at school, but kept it to himself out of fear. So, when Christopher saw his father speak and faced different situations, he looked like a big hero to him and dreamed of being like him and to become a good entrepreneur.

Carlos put away his backpack in the car and sent a message to Cindy letting her know he had the car and would go to pick her up to go to college. Cindy was waiting at the bus stop. She was leaning against a sign wearing a red dress and loose blond hair. Her smile gave away that she saw him before he blew the horn. She got in and continued to Los Angeles University.

The university was known as L.A.U. and was near the residential area of Westwood. It was one of the architectural wonders of Los Angeles since it was built in 1890 and its location was unbeatable. Carlos worked there a few days a week to pay for college, while Cindy did the same with her work at the restaurant. A degree in liberal studies opened wide job opportunities in multidisciplinary areas like humanities, arts, social sciences, and natural science. The price to pay was hard work because the materials were in some cases complex and expensive and required a lot of reading and teamwork. When the mind is set to school, time passes quickly, and worries disappear for a few hours.

At noon, they met and were eating at their favorite restaurant before Cindy started work. She had the afternoon schedule, so they took advan-

tage of an hour to be together.

Carlos told her about the nightmare. He explains that he felt a request for help from John, as if he was stuck somewhere.

"It was so real. It was not like other times. I saw him in front of me and I remember he told me something like 'help me.' "

"You must not go back, you're overcoming it, it's been two weeks since your last nightmare." She took his hand as they stared in silence.

"This time it was different. He was alone as if I had found a door to communicate with him."

"I believe rehearsals with the band may have influenced to revive memories. Maybe you should ..."

"Music is everything to me, I mean, you're my Eden, and music the universe that contains it. It's like breathing. Some memories may have been activated but believe me it is different from the dreams I had before."

"Yes, I know. I did not mean you should put aside ... never mind."

"Music fills the time I cannot be with you, and now it is part of our lives. Right now, I guess it sounds like a song, every time I see you in my mind a melody resonates. I feel my life is tied to music more than I could imagine. But also, in the worst of times."

She embraced him and fell silent. When they finished lunch, he took her to work. They were five minutes away with the vehicle. He dropped her off and returned to the University where he was an assistant in the technology area. Carlos got along well enough with the technology although it was not his main passion. Thanks to that work he could finance his studies, his band and help with some expenses at home. He knew his father sacrificed daily and his mother was engaged to carry out the home, which he should not be a burden but more of an aid.

Six hours passed, quickly. During the afternoon, his phone messages were diagramming the day's activities. At the end of the day he would stop by the Help Center to bring some donations that he had managed to retrieve. Before going there, he would pick up Cindy, who had joined the cause and enjoyed sharing with Carlos those moments when they interacted with those who needed help but also because it was a legacy of John who was the one who took him first and had taught him what it meant helping others. While driving, Carlos remembered when he told John that he had clothes that no longer needed and that he did not want to throw away. John said he had the answer and went to look for those clothes. Carlos thought he would go to a fair to sell, but when they stopped at the Help Center several ideas crossed his head, without being entirely convinced. Upon entering, several people came out to greet John and took the opportunity to introduce Carlos. It was the first cold autumn and was starting to get chilly. When John was distributing clothes among those who had spent the night there, he felt a big emotion inside. He met several families and some people who had lost everything leaving them helpless in life. There was a nucleus together where they could feel safe. The impact that Carlos received was so great that wanted to go find clothes that he still used to give to them. Then he brought blankets and some clothes from his siblings for resident children. John put together a library with books that were no longer needed at the university.

The Help Center housed about forty people made up of several families. The price of rent plus the inflation caused a strong impact on the most vulnerable social sectors. A monthly subsidy for medicines and food was given so they could have food to eat.

The car stopped at the traffic lights and Carlos snapped out of it after the honking of other vehicles. He was going to find Cindy who had joined as an assistant and used her free time to work with Carlos and Mrs. Grace, one of the homeless people who was there from the beginning and did the cooking. The couple had gotten a TV, a radio and a few computers which he managed to obtain since the university changed to a new system. He stopped the car at the corner where Cindy worked. Whenever he went to find her, he remembered the first time he saw her as he felt the freshness of her smile and eyes. After a few minutes, she left waving her arms from the door. She got inside his car and headed to the Help Center.

III. HELP CENTER

The Help Center is a 3-story-building that was home to families after one of the most devastating tornadoes hit one of the nearby states. It was a place where many homeless people could spend the night and have a hot meal, especially on cold winter nights where temperatures dropped significantly. While receiving substantial assistance in terms of paying for medicines and food, there was always the need for donations.

Each of those who came to the Center contributed in some way, usually helping with some tasks such as cleaning the place or doing the dishes. Some people actively worked after losing their families by being forgotten by them or retired. At the Help Center they found a second home and assumed roles such as Mrs. Grace, an African American woman with a smile as wide as her apron. She had lost her husband many years ago and his son had gone to live in New Orleans and never called her. So, she sought to have the grandchildren that her family didn't share and enjoyed making cakes for the children.

Mr. Rodney was a veteran who served his country as a doctor during the war. He was responsible for the general maintenance and safeguarding medications, inventory of supplies and assigning doses of medication to patients as needed. He was a tall man with marked features and his mustache made him look more serious but was very sweet when children greeted him. After the war he never married or had children. He spent his time doing what he did best.

A group of people were responsible for the administrative tasks of the Center and to receive donations.

The couple arrived at 7 pm and parked the car in front of the building. Upon entering Rodney came to help, courteously taking the bag Cindy was carrying.

"Let me help you, ma'am," he said as he moved to grab the bags.

"Thanks Rod," she replied.

"Do you want us to leave the bags in the storage room?" asked the young man as he carried some bags as he patted the shoulder of the giant.

"Yes, tomorrow I'll tell the boys to help me separate and distribute all these," Rod said.

"Okay, you're the boss!" Cindy waved indicating that her phone was ringing.

The men dropped the bags and set them on a large table.

"We have a new member, a man named Frank Jackson," said the giant as they climbed the stairs. "I'll introduce you to him."

"Is he a former famous blues musician?" asked Carlos as he hummed "boom boom boom boom."

"He was discharged from hospital and sent for social assistance, was in intensive care for more than a month."

"What happened?" asked Carlos in a curious tone.

"Apparently, he was blind because of an attack or something related to a kidnapping," he said, with an air of mystery.

Carlos's eyes widened and he felt something burning inside him. He climbed the stairs rapidly and when he got to the top his phone started ringing.

"Hello?"

"Hi Carlos, I'm Rick," he said.

"How are you, doctor?" while trying to calm the sudden agitation. Rick Thomas was Carlos's professor at the university and liked Carlos for his genuine personality and generosity.

"Sorry to call you at this hour, I need to ask you a favor. I wouldn't call if it was not important. Are you far from Santa Monica?"

"I'm about six kilometers. Tell me how I can be of help," he responded with intrigue, while Cindy crossed words with Rod.

"Look, we had a problem with some medications that should have arrived today at Children's Miracle. I had one of the laboratories give me five boxes after an ordeal, the problem is that I need to catch a flight. Can you pick them up?"

"Yes, send me your address, I'm driving a car, I'll be there in twenty minutes."

"Thank you, I'm coming home. The person who was supposed to come had an accident, and you are my student with my absolute confidence. I'll send you my address."

"I'll be there soon while you prepare your suitcase."

"There, I sent you the address. See you in a bit."

"Okay," and hung up as Cindy started coming towards him.

Carlos put his hands on her shoulders letting her know they had to go and went to talk to Rod.

"Rod, something came up. May I speak with this man tomorrow?"

"Of course. Come back and I'll introduce you to Frank."

"I'll call you tomorrow to schedule an appointment," he said, as he stretched his hand to say goodbye.

"Bye, Carlos. Thanks for the donations."

"Say bye to Grace for me," and he went to the door next to Cindy who waved her arm from a distance.

They drove to the beach area of Santa Monica. They talked about the call Rick made and the medicines for the Children's Miracles. They were listening to a rock radio station.

"Can you imagine if music could heal the sick? I mean, when you hear a song you like, you feel your body generates some energy. If we had the power to heal all those children" Carlos said, as he was driving.

"You know that plants improve their appearance when they are playing classical music."

"True, a few weeks ago in class we saw the case of a scientist who experiments with water, playing different types of music and freezing the water. Then with a microscope, it showed how crystals were generated as kaleidoscopes depending on the sound and the style of music. When putting soothing music, water showed as a beautiful figurine, but when putting something more intense water seemed like sharp needles."

"Not that I do not believe," she said, with a surprised face, "that means if you play heavy metal horns will come out and the water will start shaking," and both started laughing.

"And why not?" Carlos responded, "music is a vibration, vibration affects things. Atoms are constantly vibrating, and the number of oscillations of the molecules in a second, it's the frequency! A crystal glass can be broken when the sound emitting is the same frequency as that of the glass. Dr. Rick Thomas is an expert in that field."

"True, they even had fallen bridges due to oscillation" she said shaking her hands.

"I dream of something great with the music. I've always wanted that and the music we create with EZ Door to reach any frontier. It can reach other galaxies through a space capsule!"

"The EZ Door will be live on Saturn" Cindy commented like a concert announcer.

"Not bad at all!" he said and they both laughed as they continued the journey to the residential area of Santa Monica.

Dr. Rick Thomas lives in a very modern building overlooking the sea. He is a man who is in his 50's. He has a tall and slender figure that gives him the air of one of those scientists who seem to levitate in the air. He has several master's degrees and a Ph.D. in Physics and Sound Engineering.

The house appeared impressive, with two tall palm trees that seemed to guard the entrance. It was structured in two floors and had a privileged view of Palisades Park and contrasted with the sky and the sea. Modern architecture noted many amenities and technological features of the place. The couple parked the car and headed down to the door to a large protective grille garage door. Looking up a broad balcony where plants were placed to decorate the location.

They rang the bell and a voice invited them to enter. Then the door opened, and they went inside the house. They entered a large hall decorated by paintings and a fountain. The lights seemed to guide them toward the central hall. They followed the path and there appeared Dr. Rick Thomas, wearing a white linen suit and a light blue shirt. Some wrinkles denoting certain weariness on his face.

"Thanks for coming," he said as he stretched his hand to greet him firmly, "and you must be Cindy" and he approached her with a kiss on the cheek.

"Make yourselves at home, have a seat," responded Rick.

He led the way to Cindy who sat in one of the chairs next to Carlos. She noticed how big the apartment was which had a large wardrobe, dark red on color with a silver Greek inscription and a large mirror. On the right wing there was a piano and a series of classical guitars hanging on the wall. The large window offered a magnificent view of the beach with the sun descending like a pillar on the horizon.

"We do not want to take too much of your time," said Carlos, respectfully.

"We have time, in twenty minutes a taxi will take me to the airport, it will only take a few minutes to prepare everything. If you want something to drink help yourself. If you excuse me, I'll be right back," he said, as he left.

Cindy put her hand on Carlos' shoulder to relax him a bit. Carlos was resting his back until Rick brought back styrofoam boxes.

"Here you go. Next week I will pay a visit to the children. I didn't make it last time, so I hope to compensate in some way. By the way Carlos, Rod told me of your contribution in recent months and I am very proud of you." Carlos nodded gratefully for the compliment with a nod, looking down.

"You have a very nice house," Cindy interrupted with a smile, "that boy in the picture, is he your son?" while directing her gaze to the picture frames located on top of one of the furniture pieces.

It was a boy about seven years old with a blue surfboard, and black and yellow beach clothes.

Rick changed his face for a split second, then smiled as if nothing happened.

"Yes," he said while drawing a look of nostalgia.

"The view is very picturesque, the Palisades Park is one of our favorite places," Carlos said. He felt they asked something they should not have asked and continued "let's take these boxes so that we can go to the movies, remember?"

"Sometimes the memories play tricks on me," Rick said looking down, keeping his face calm, "Eddie was his name. We fought to the end against the cancer. It was many years ago." Then, he looked at Carlos and said, "He would have been your age."

"We did not want ..." said Carlos trying to be polite and rose as Rick looked at him calmly.

"Everything is fine. If I did not have confidence in you, I would have not told you," watching him calmly, "You two make a cute couple. I heard a lot about your girlfriend's visits to the Help Center."

"It's a good way to collaborate with the community and to be together sharing activities other than music or college."

Cindy took Carlos by the arms.

"I have to go see your band one day," and before Carlos could answer, Cindy said,

"You are in front of a rock star," and she winked at Carlos.

"Well, Rick it is not so," as he looked at Cindy.

"I've seen some posters advertising your shows. I got to go see you, it is a pending matter."

"Yes! Saturday he will be performing live," said the girl staring back at Carlos.

"It's been a while since I've been to a concert, if it was not for my trip I would stop by, I know I could use some air. When I was young, I also played in a band. I played the guitar and the keyboard," he said pointing toward the musical instruments room, "I hope that the entry is not restricted to older musicians."

"No way! There is always room for Old School!" Carlos ranted, "... too much responsibility. Now we have to do a show under pressure, we have to be sure to shine. Afterwards, you got to tell me more about the band you had!"

"I will, I'll make sure to bring some tomatoes to throw at you if I don't like your show, as it was done in my time." The couple burst into laughter at the comment.

Carlos took the meds while Cindy thanked Rick.

The man walked them to the door where they parted. The couple got in the car and set off back to the Children's Miracle with medications.

On the way Cindy tune in a station transmitting music from the eighties, a station used to play in the restaurant.

"Only a few hours before you return to play with the band. I am very excited to see you on stage again." Said Cindy very excited.

"I'm pretty nervous, you know? If it were not for you and the guys in the band, I think I would have thrown it all away."

"Sometimes it is hard to accept it, but music means a lot to you," responded Cindy.

"I just do not feel quite ready. It's like there's something holding me back."

"It's the nightmares, I think you should go ahead. John would have wished it."

"Yes, I think it affects me I just want justice. Rod told me about a new member at the Help Center apparently was kidnapped. I will go see him tomorrow before the rehearsal."

"If you want to I can go with you to the Center. I want to talk to Grace about that recipe for the brownies. Let's leave these things and go see that movie," said Cindy as she examined her phone messages.

"Yes ma'am! ... *más rápido que un avión, más rápido que una locomotora...*" Carlos said in perfect Spanish singing the voice of the program he used to watch as a child.

The car went through the city, which looked like a perfect formation of stars and glitter. The streets looked like a luminous pearls necklace by the number of vehicles. The spring festival celebrated all day, in a city where lights never went out. After several minutes of travel they arrived at the Children's Miracle, a building that looked like a huge rectangular box made of glass. Tinted windows were carefully selected to filter out ultraviolet rays. The bright rooms with warm light created patient care and containment environment. The clinic was open to society, and offered medical care to children of all ages as well as care for those who were terminal. This sector was located on the first floor.

Children's Miracle was sponsored by a foundation headed by a successful entrepreneur whose origin was presumed South American named, Walter R. His donations kept the place under working conditions and at a cost so low it was virtually free providing a solution for many disadvantaged sectors.

He was a prominent figure at a social level and he also helped several of the Help Centers that were scattered in the city, including the one Carlos volunteered.

Each end of the year, the billionaire sent gifts and through his foundation, collection of food and clothing were organized. His popularity had reached the ears of several politicians who were trying to add him to their campaigns, however, he stayed away.

The couple entering the building and before he could leave the boxes, one of the nurses carried a child in a wheelchair whose hair had fallen out due to the chemotherapy. When he saw the couple, greeted them by moving his thin arms. Cindy was very heart-broken yet managed to overcome answering with a smile. Carlos did the same by moving his hands to cheer him up.

After a short entry and admission procedure of the boxes, the couple left the building.

"Hey beautiful, are you okay? It looks like something bad has happened," as the girl lifted her face from the ground.

"I was thinking of that child, his smile when greeted, and everything he must be going through."

"Yes, and you know that he will be well taken care of here," pausing as he squeezed her hand slightly.

"I wish I could do something, I do not know what, even if it were to be reading a book."

"It's a pretty good idea, we can arrange a visit, what do you think?" he said holding her.

"I feel better now," Cindy said with a gleam in her eyes and immediately merged into a kiss and hug as if the world did not exist at all.

IV. CONSPIRACY

The ride to the airport brought back memories of his son. Little Eddie was all that was good in a child who brushed perfection with a cheerful and curious personality. He represented his pride and his passion, the perfect nexus with his wife who had achieved a harmonious relationship with the arrival of the new family member. The first years of his life helped him understand how fragile people are and reach out to the Children's Miracle since its inception. His life only seemed full of successes and joys. Like a tsunami, everything was washed away.

It was a year of struggle where everything became a crippling battle to save the life of Eddie. Just a few months later, his family had become a mere memory. The work to cure illnesses kept him alive, feeding an obsessive spirit wanting to reverse what happened by saving other lives. His wife did not have the same strength and left him a few months later.

Rick remembered to turn on his phone. The vibration of his cell phone caught his attention while traveling in the taxi. He left it charging and now he was receiving all the miss calls and messages.

The phone rang before he could finish reading the messages.

"Hello?" he said looking at the reflection of the stars at the sea in the distance.

"Hi Rick, at last I managed to find you!" said a female voice with an oriental accent.

Ying was Rick's secretary, a young Chinese woman working together toward their goals for a couple of years when both joined SkyGold Technologies. Her thin and stylized features made her look like a porcelain doll, and her quiet personality but actively and effectively generated in Rick the trust and backup he needed without worrying about bureaucratic issues. The relationship was very casual without overstepping the limits of respect. Rick liked that because she looked more like a friend than a secretary.

"The flight was rescheduled for late next week due to the hurricanes," she said in a soft, unhurried tone, "and there's more ... taking advantage of this unexpected delay Rex asked me to schedule a meeting for Saturday."

"Oh no!" he said suddenly, "... ok ... ok," Rick stuttered as if it had rained a bag of bricks.

"I am sending you the memo."

"Thanks, Ying," said as he showed the taxi driver how to change the route, "I don't know what I'd do without you."

"It was nothing Rick. Have a good night," responded Ying.

"Goodbye," he said, relaxing on the seat of the taxi.

The phone vibrated again with the announcement of the appointment and a letter from the laboratory. His sharp fingers accepted the meeting, and immediately opened the received files folder. The mail was related to one of the tests that had been scheduled. In the end, the system issued a report of results and sent by email automatically. Quickly analyze the information and saw that the overall average indicated a 100% compatibility. "I got it," he thought internally as the taxi approached his home.

"This weekend I will have a lot of work to do," he thought as the car was moving at the closing of the night.

SkyGold Technologies was an imposing glass jungle. Some called it the Louvre of technology for its architecture. It was located on an extensive campus about one kilometer from the city. The perimeter was closed with electrified security bars contrasting with the landscape of trees surrounding the complex. A classic black car stopped at the entrance and a heavily armed security guard waved at him to advance. He lowered the window slowly and greeted the guard.

"Good day, Peter. Has Dr. Rex arrived yet?"

"Good morning, Dr. Rick. Yes, about an hour ago. He seemed somewhat annoyed because he almost hit me with his car. It seems he's

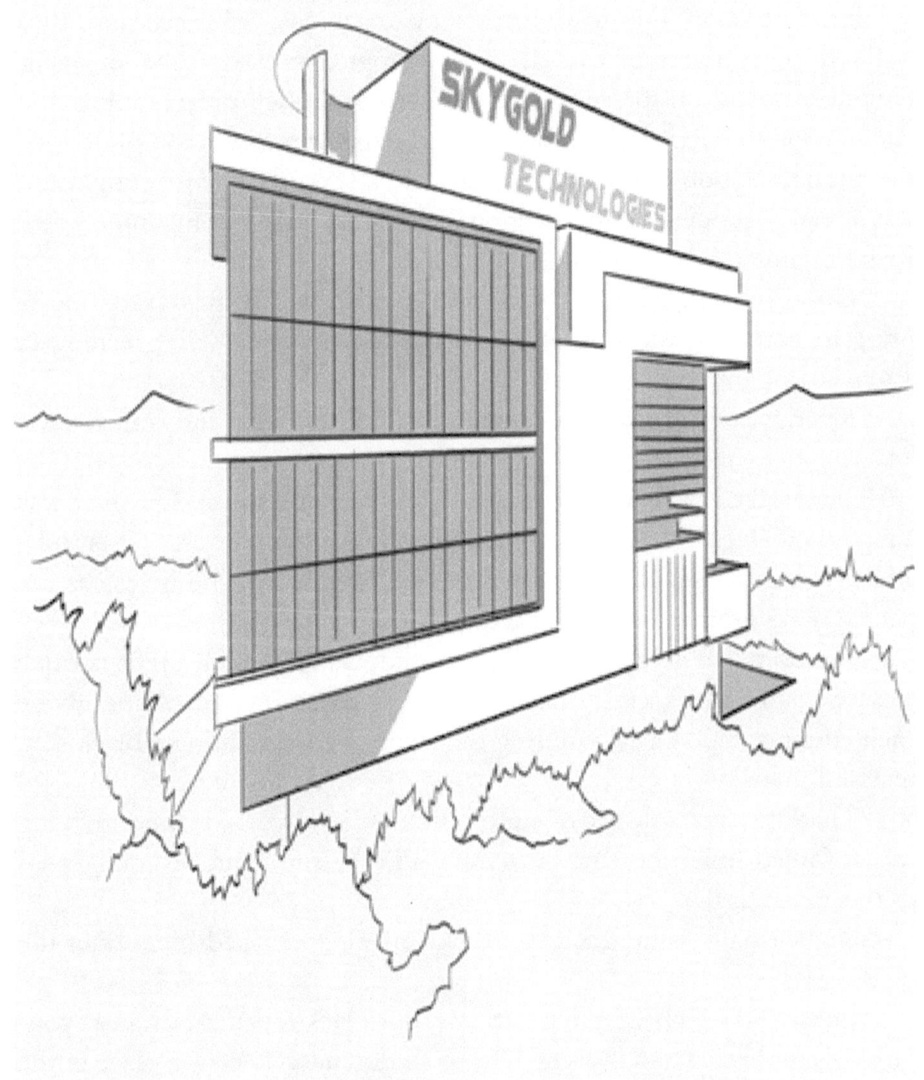
SKYGOLD
TECHNOLOGIES

having a bad day!"

"Mmm... it seems we will have a busy morning. Don't let that affect your day," he said, politely as the guard approached him with a sensor for fingerprint verification.

"Well, good thing everything else is going great," said the guard as he rested a hand on his waist.

Rick rested his hand and the gate began to open. The guard went back to his booth waving at Rick. The main road was illuminated by a colorful rainbow due to the irrigation machines. After parking, Rick went to the entrance of one of the buildings that was on the left-wing. He put his hand on the sensor, and then a new fingerprint reading, and digital code to enter the complex. A three-meter hall was the prelude to the building. Upon entering the main hall, he spotted the meeting room was already occupied. After greeting the security guards, Ying intercepted Rick bringing a folder to him.

"Good morning, Rick. This is the agenda that Dr. Rex asked me to bring to you. The meeting will begin in ten minutes." He greeted her afterwards.

"Really, you're always one step ahead," he said, and she smiled shyly lowering her gaze.

They walked by a wide staircase to the meeting room. On their way Ying was telling him that the folder contained a number of points to be addressed and a schedule on the project. Apparently, the investors expected news on the progress and due dates.

The room had no curtains, and the windows were made up of opaque glass. Sensors and security cameras were located on the ceiling above each entrance hall. Upon entering the room, a man wearing a black suit, received them.

"That's punctuality, Rick," ranted Rex as he waved. He went to Ying with a forced smile showing his teeth, "and the sun from east enlightens us this morning."

Ying formally saluted Rex, as Rick smiled, and asked him about the meeting.

"I have the results of the prototype, but I lack most importantly your progress report." Then inviting him to sit down while taking place at the end of the table.

"The board is asking for a progress report of the project," Rex said in a tone of little importance, "there are several million at stake, but just like you, I want this to work no matter what."

"We are very close," said interrupting him, "also the forces of nature were responsible for changing my weekend plans."

"Does someone want coffee?" Ying said, briefly interrupting.

"Expresso," Rex said, pointing with his index finger.

"Some water for me. Thank you," Rick said as he sat in the middle of the table looking at Rex.

Ying walked out as the men stayed silent for a few seconds.

At the opposite end, a curved monitor showing a screen with the company logo. Rex took the floor just as Rick was going to speak.

"It's been one year since the start of the project. Costs have exceeded the 25% initial estimates. Our investors are demanding news and what better than a field test."

"Well, we passed the prototype stage with which we can do. It was achieved possessing ergonomic flexibility and the micro engineering team finished adjustments on the suit," Rick responded.

"At this point cost is not an issue. Either way we need that equipment ready." Rex said, vehemently looking at Rick.

Rick looked at the man trying to hide a smile.

"So? I imagine you have something else to say." Ying came in with a tray of coffee and water just when Rex was talking and took a seat. Rick thanked her by giving her a wink before taking a sip.

"Let me show you on the screen."

Rick connected a type of tablet to the network and turned on a curved screen that occupied one side of the room. The images showed graphs with curves and a human figure like an exoskeleton. They were going through waves, graphs, and curves with red, blue, and green colors. Some came from a network of satellites.

"As you know, sound is a way to anticipate the moods of human beings. Somehow, it affects the way we perceive the environment, nature, and the world. All those 'vibrations' invade our body; in some cases, they are assimilated, and in others rejected. We were having problems because we lacked to consider one of the most important components of all," explained Rick.

"Interesting ... so?" asked Rex with a lot of anxiety. Rick continued.

"Emotions are the key! This in turn affects our daily lives and our way of life." Rex stared at him letting him know to close the idea.

"The tests we did with the team placing them in different parts of the town, paid off! All synchronized, we found a mix of very interesting frequencies. In some areas where crimes happened, believe it or not, are chaotic places that seem to unleash such violence. In other cases, the quietest places led tranquility and calmness, and even nightclubs, increased drug use or violence was measured with the spectrum of emotions," as he spoke some images were showing different parts of the city dyed with warm, muted colors and darkness. "We tried high intensity and sudden loud noises that causes people's feelings of fear that prepares them to either fight or flight."

"In short, the use of the suit is 100% compatible!" Rick said, swiftly anticipating any interruption.

Rex opened his eyes, as if Rick pulled an ace from his sleeve.

"I can review the critical points. We got it, Rex!"

Ying tried to hide her smile looking down.

"You had an ace up your sleeve!" Rex said.

"Yes, I do. The key ingredient will be music and sound. The suit was synchronized with the headphones and connected to the satellite. It can access abundant data without limits!"

"Have you tried the amplifier wave?" Rex asked eager wondering for news.

"Just the amplifier module, which was used in the tests. That was exactly what we transfer to the suit. It made perfect synchronization with the neural network of who uses it! Even the power meter can indicate when to recharge. Lithium modules give a range of 72 hours. Of course, it can be improved."

"Then we can begin the Alpha Phase. It is no longer a beta version of the suit. What do you think Rick?" asked Rex in a high tone.

"I cannot wait to be able to use it in front of hundreds of people. The potential to cure various diseases is huge! This will go beyond the magnetic therapy! I just have to work a little harder in this field."

"There is no time Rick. I have to present it this week to the investors."

"Wait, we're there, give me a few more weeks ... I'm working so that it can contain the cells. We are one step away from reducing tumors and other illnesses!"

"This week we move forward as scheduled," responded Rex in a demanding voice.

"Listen, we need a little more time, the potential is huge, I cannot figure out what can be achieved with the suit as it is. I mean, the artificial intelligence node can make the suit learn and incorporate new vibrations, but I cannot determine whether it is stable or if the suit has implications!"

"Then we'll discover them along the way. I need you to prepare everything to take it to the field test."

"A week, just one week that is all I ask!" Rick said fully animated, but without raising his voice.

"Remember, how are things now? Or should I isolate you from the project so that you can understand it?" said Rex in a high tone.

"You can't be serious!" said Rick rising from his chair.

"Of course, I can!" Rex answered yelling that left Rick speechless.

"Prepare the equipment. We will start the tests on Monday," Rex said, like a dry bark, and immediately the man stood up and left the room with an unfriendly face.

Rick was stunned. He turned to Ying.

"I would rather deal with the hurricanes. Please cancel the flight for the moment." Ying looked at him and nodded.

The woman left the room leaving Rick slumped in his chair as if he had lost a fight by knock out.

The relationship between Dr. Rex and Rick Thomas had started five years ago. The first project they had worked on, managed to help children with acoustic hiccups, and had been implemented in the Children's Miracle.

Rick has the creative brain, but Rex ripped the rewards. At the beginning Rick maintained a low profile. However, with the new project, co-existence began to have its frictions. Now, he had to respond to Rex.

Rick left the meeting room and entered his office and sat in his chair while his brain sought to understand how the relationship was broken. His desk had a few monitors which were connected to the satellite network where hundreds of lines crossing the entire continent were seen. He began preparing the synchronization of networks to incorporate them into the main program of the suit. The task was almost automated and only needed to compile the program to have its own autonomy. The firmware can be updated automatically and added with each new network or new sound drivers. The development was complex, and a job well done noticeable when the green indicator marked the completion of the process. It was done.

He examined the report history. Final testing consisted of an emulation of the neural network with a sound interface. The prototype was similar to a headset, adjusted and adapted to the ear of those who used the suit. The music was played when connected to various sensors wirelessly, although it was difficult to say exactly what else the suit is capable of doing as they had not tested it completely.

The phone vibrated. It was a message from Ying that said, *"Come see me in the parking lot."*

He would have called her, but he understood it must be something very important, something that no one else was supposed to listen to.

"Ok, five minutes," he replied and left the phone on his desk.

Before leaving he left a secured copy of the documents. When he got to the parking Ying was already there. She seemed nervous and restless and moved as if expecting that someone might suddenly appear.

When she saw Rick coming toward her she said,

"Let's get in the car," and immediately Ying opened the car door leaving the door open so he could climb on the other side. He nodded surprised by her attitude.

"Tell me what this is all about. If you wanted to go out we could go have lunch." He said with a smile at her, but she had a serious face.

"Something is wrong with the project ..." he wanted to interrupt, her but she raised her hand to indicate to let her speak.

"A while back I went down through the emergency exit to leave stuff in my car. I was about to get in when I noticed I got something in my shoe, that's when I turned to remove it and clean it. At that moment I heard Rex's voice." Ying said, with increasingly serious face. Rick changed his face too.

"I don't like eavesdropping, however, being alone I was petrified. Rex was talking to someone who called himself, 'Kacique', and said that the homeless people were ready for the following experiments and that the suit was ready."

"Are you sure it was Rex who was talking?" Rick said with his eyes open and completely surprised and shocked.

"Yes, it was him. That's when the situation terrified me, as I squatted. He moved to where I was, I was afraid he could see me or hear me even breathe. His voice was evil, and sadistic. He gave an address in downtown Los Angeles and was going to communicate in an hour from the location. Then shortly, he turned back and re-entered the building. I stayed a few minutes shaking, and that's when I sent you the message. Since that time, I moved to the parking lot and waited for you."

"Ok, how are you now?" asked Rick, as his hand rested on her shoulder.

"Horrible," Ying said, as she was tense as a bow.

"You should try to calm down. Do you remember the address that Rex mentioned?"

"Yes," she said, holding her breath trembling.

"Ying, thank you for your confidence, and I need to ask you to do something very important. We will go on as if nothing has happened. There's something very odd about all this and I need to find out. I've made a backup copy of the project files. While we have scheduled backups, I uploaded the adjustments and was leaving everything ready to launch the final phase."

Rick's phone vibrated. It was Rex.

"Hello," Rick said, as he motioned for silence to Ying.

"Where are you? I stopped by your office and you were not there."

"Hello Rex, right now I'm ...busy. Have you ever gone to the restroom?"

"Sorry, does the power stage of the suit use batteries that charge automatically?"

"I still need to adapt one of the modules."

"I understand that will be ready tomorrow, right? It should be tested outdoors to evaluate possible interference."

"Perfect. So shall be."

"OK, goodbye."

"Goodbye."

He went to Ying asking her to accompany him to his office. As they were getting out of the car he said:

"I want to ask you something very important. I need to get the project information for any eventuality. When the transfer is done you must unplug the device and take it. I will also give backups so that they can't be restored and track down the suit via satellite networks. Meanwhile, I'll see what kind of experiments Rex is doing."

Ying nodded, and together they entered back on the building.

V. Capoeira

The spacious bright room of the Capoeira HLP housed about 15 young people of different ages. There were women and men, from different heights, and approximately equal ages were mixed together. Alternating their feet, they were jumping from one to another, and one of them began with the attack while the other jumped back and defended. The rest performed the same movements with synchronized harmony.

Combined techniques to the rhythm of the music that filled the room, and sometimes performed cartwheels that could apply to certain attacks.

Carlos felt alive and full of energy doing what he loved. That Saturday started out his day practicing at the local Capoeira HLP. A middle-aged man approached Carlos while another young man was practicing. His physique was medium size and possessed incredible agility for someone his age. He explained a movement of arms and then sweeps that could be applied in the technique. The other young man imitated, and the instructor slowed him down to correct him. Carlos ran back and moved his arms with great speed and agility. Then bent down and with a sweep of his leg gave half a turn. The instructor smiled to confirm the proper use of the technique.

He separated the group and explained that the exercise consisted of hiding from the adversary of an attack at that right time. Practitioners wore black pants, and white, or yellow shirts. It made them look less formal to keep them from the conventionality of martial arts. Carlos turned to the man asking, "Jim, tell me how to make the enemy not see your feet. Depending on the position I stand surely it can be detected whether throwing a kick or a punch."

"You can keep up with your movements and attacks when you see fit. Thus, you achieve control over yourself and nobody can anticipate your movements."

"It does not seem so simple."

"It is not," said the man again capturing the attention of the whole group explaining a number of new moves.

Jim was the capoeira instructor and was the founder of the school that opens Saturday morning. The schedule was enviable because it allows you to have the rest of the day. Nothing better to end the week with something you like.

The instructor separated them again into teams of two to re-run the steps, dance, attack, defense and lateral flips. Some of the more advanced participants performed a backflip. Carlos still could not get that mastered, however, the speed of his defense and attack stood out from the rest of the group.

He performed a sweeping technique and his opponent fell to the ground. Carlos held out his hand to help his opponent get back up, and continued to practice.

Jim noticed Carlos getting better in a very short time, and had gained great skills that surprised him. Some of the older students have not yet mastered the technique and saw how the young apprentice was growing rapidly. It made the class take more dynamism, but he also made mistakes and it was there when he collided with reality.

Carlos felt happy while his body responded to the movements of the rhythms of music. It was his sanctuary, his joy on Saturday mornings. That night he played with EZ Door, and had decided there was only one way to ease his anxiety and it was to practice harder.

Carlos was still feeling the pressure from John's memories, and capoeira was a way to achieve balance within himself. Those nightmares, those dreams that seemed to connect with his friend, made him feel guilty for not being able to save him, not been strong enough to fight off the attackers. After months of training, the muscles of Carlos looked strengthened, and his resistance improved.

The music started as Jim approached by choosing three attackers. The group formed a circle, and when everything seemed to be a new lesson, Carlos was called to the center. Without a word, the teacher indicated by signs to the attackers to go around him and started clapping while other students who were at the outer ring mimicked him applauding to the beat of the music generating more intensity and energy.

Jim told the fighters to maneuver hand and feet attacks. He went to Carlos and covered his eyes with a handkerchief. The music mixed the melodies and the applause from the other students.

"Defend your position," someone whispered in his ear.

He felt the energy vibrating inside of him during the class.

The first order of the instructor was for the attackers to disperse and begin to attack from different directions. Carlos started at the beginning to make out of the silhouettes surrounding him until he received the first blow destabilizing his position. The second attack was frontal and blocked it with his hands quickly. The attacks were happening quickly, without giving him a break and the young man turned trying not to lose the rhythm of music. A kick landed on his leg and slammed his knee to the ground. His first intention was to remove the bandage and attack but did not have time because he received another blow this time on his right shoulder. It was not strong enough to hurt him but to enough to make him furious.

"Self-control!" shouted the teacher.

"Will!" shouted Jim again while Carlos stood up and continued to move by pacing the music.

"Perception!" was the last word Carlos heard and started a series of strikes after each musical beat, in sync with the applause Carlos was able to block with his arms and legs.

It seemed to have some logic as if anticipating where would the new kick come from. It was there when he jumped and threw a kick that caught the blow of one of the attackers and left stunned because was not expected that he could defend and attack simultaneously.

The other two attackers pounced at the same time as Carlos swept off the floor one of them and fell back.

Jim made sure that every time one of the attackers was hit by an attack from Carlos, another would alternate. The latter had managed to jump back but did not manage to hit him. It only took one sidekick to take him out of action. The applause and shouts came immediately. Other colleagues cheered and waved as the class ended. Even those who had been defeated by Carlos approached him to congratulate him. Just a couple of older students were jealous and laughed moving away from the scene.

At the end of the class, he went to the bus stop where he checked his phone. There was a message from Ethan arranging the schedule for the night. He boarded the bus to take him home carrying a bag with his training clothes.

When he sat down, it seemed that the adrenaline was still flowing, his fingers moved swiftly as he swept the bridge of his imaginary guitar. He put on his hood and leaned against the window while sending a message to Roy to say he should not take more than the drumsticks. It was one of the few times that their instruments were not needed. Off the bus he crossed the street and while walking flexed his legs as if thrusting and following a rhythm only he could hear. Approaching the driveway of his house Christopher was sitting on the sidewalk with his head resting on his hands.

"Hi Chris. What's wrong?" said Carlos stooping to see the child's face.

"Nothing, I want to be alone, that's all," Chris said with a teary voice.

Carlos looked around but did not spot anyone. He went to his brother resting a hand on his shoulder.

"Chris, I'm your older brother, remember? Have you had problems at school again?"

Christopher looked down as his eyes filled with tears.

"I want to be like dad ..." he said, with watery eyes. His voice cracked, and every word was a difficult mission to complete, "he knows how to put things...in its...place."

"And you too! Tell me. I want to help you" said Carlos.

"There are some older kids that bother me because I'm fat," Christopher said wiping away tears as his eyes filled with rage, "and they took pictures of me to ridicule me."

"They are fools. You can't let them win. Look, you remember that picture mom took of me where I come out with a funny face, we all have something that we can't escape, however the solution is to learn to laugh at ourselves" said Carlos in a joking manner.

"... and they hit me ..." Christopher said, with his eyes down again and clenched fists.

Carlos's face hardened to such disclosure.

"When did this happened? ... Is that the reason why you were so quiet yesterday? ... that is serious Chris."

"They threatened to upload photos to social media. It was Thursday, when I was changing after gym class that they entered. They threw the restroom paper basket on top of me. I began to fight them off, but I got hit in the chest and fell against the lockers." Christopher lift up his t-shirt which showed his bruises.

"This will not stay like that little brother. I just need you to talk to mom and dad. They have to know."

"But ..."

"No buts," and he hugged him, "I assure you this will not stay that way."

"There is more, one of them said his father will kill us if I say something, and I think it could be true because I was warned he was in jail," responded Christopher.

"Well before killing anyone he must deal with me. Come on, after lunch we'll talk with mom and dad."

Carlos stood and stretched his hand to the child. He looked at him and after a few seconds he got up too.

Upon entering his home, Kimberly was watching a tv program where participants competed singing and dancing. Her mother was sitting on the couch watching the program and occasionally checked her cell phone to find the songs she listened to for building her playlist.

"Hello family," Carlos said in a tone lower than the music. The women saluted and he waved to his mother catching her attention. Kimberly watched him and took the remote to decrease the volume and Carlos motioned for her to stay watching the program. Christopher was very close to his brother still with watery eyes. When his mother saw him they went to the kitchen taking the child by the hand.

"What happened? Are you ok?" asked Araceli.

"Yes, mom, I think we need to talk when dad comes home. Chris has ..." at that time Christopher looked at his brother as if to prevent him from going further.

"Listen to Chris, the only way to solve problems in the family is by talking about them." She looked at Carlos and her gaze conveyed security. Her gesture indicated that she would take care of the situation.

"What happened son?" Araceli said, stroking the child's head.

"Some kids at school hit me and ... threa ...ten ... to kill ... us ..." he stammered the last words as his eyes filled with tears. She hugged him and let him show his emotions and after a while, he calmed down.

"Look, none of that will happen. I need you to tell us all the details. Dad will come in a bit and we'll talk to him. These bullies will no longer bother you."

"The father of one of them is a criminal ... he was in jail and ..."

"And will remain in prison if he dares to harm us," she said with confidence. Carlos sat beside his mother.

"You are very brave brother. There are many children who stay silent, and their parents are not aware of these things," said the young man.

"That's right, and it is a big mistake not to talk about it because it creates ghosts in your mind and you are filled with fear. Your family is here to help you and we will," she said in a firm but calm tone.

The sound of the car in the garage was the sign that Robert had arrived. They heard the front door open and his hoarse voice greeted Kimberly. Araceli could not help but smile with a twinkle in her eyes when she heard him talk.

She got up and went to look. Meanwhile, Christopher had managed to calm down and his eyes no longer pointed at the ground. Carlos was standing next to Christopher made gestures of their parents in love when his mother left, managing to get a couple of smiles from his brother.

"Why do people act that way?" the boy asked his brother.

"In life, we come across people of all kinds. Some act in good faith and others simply do not. There are people who look good on the outside, and when you meet them, turn out to be quite the opposite. I happened to see in the Help Center many families who live unprotected, homeless and how people treat them differently and contemptuously for being different, but they are still struggling to have a future."

Robert then entered with Araceli.

"Hello boys," he said, and as he opened the door Araceli helping him with some bags and boxes of food.

"Hi, dad!" they replied in unison.

"I brought some Chinese food," and he made a gesture stretching his eyes that made the sad face of the child became an irrepressible laugh, "Let's eat and then we'll talk to let your big brother rest. Tonight, you need to work on your presentation and should be concentrating on it, isn't that right son?" he said, winking at Carlos who shook his head in approval.

"Your mother told me something, and I want you to know son you are not alone."

"Of course, you're not," said Carlos, resting his hand on his brother's shoulder. Robert nodded with a smile and opened the door so they could pass through.

Christopher sat down feeling his family was supportive and went to the dining room.

Kimberly was helping to bring the glasses to the table and Robert was taking Chinese food boxes from the bags while Carlos was helping distribute them on each place of the table. Araceli was sitting and thanked his son when he gave her his portion, she was not very devoted to Chinese food, however, the chow mein with vegetables was her favorite. Carlos sat down and took the opportunity to send a message to Cindy, "At 3 pm I will go to the Help Center." Twenty seconds later he received the reply "see you there ☺"

Family lunch was one of the rituals of the weekend. They all liked to share that special moment where some activity was planned for the evening.

"How was your exam, yesterday?" asked Robert.

"It is next week," Carlos said, looking at her mother as he started laughing. Araceli was trying to grab chopsticks for the vegetables and opened her eyes at Robert.

"Honey, he told you yesterday about a project. Surely you do not remember our anniversary date!" Robert looked at the situation while trying to remember."

"Well, I thought it was yesterday, and yes, of course, I remember the date of 'our anniversary.'" "You better remember dear, and do not forget it" she said with a sarcastic tone showing the ring on her finger.

Carlos enjoyed watching their parents have these little squabbles and liked to make his siblings laugh by tapping them with his foot under the table. After lunch, Araceli asked Kimberly to help clear the table. Carlos helped to carry some things and as the girls went to the living room he returned to his brother and father.

Robert's friendly face was serious, as serious as when John died. Christopher told without omitting details about what happened. Carlos sat listening to the end of dialogue. The boy did not cry, though he looked annoyed, frustrated, helpless as if Christopher had been transformed from a scared child into an angry one.

"This weekend I will talk to the parents of those children. If I have no answer, on Monday I will go against the school and sue them if no action is taken on this matter," he said serious but quiet.

"I am angry, dad ...I was very scared at the beginning. In fact, I was a little afraid that they might do something, and I'm also tired of hiding from those people just because they do not like the way I am."

Araceli and Kimberly joined the family reunion. Robert took a seat on the couch to leave his wife, and the girl to sit next to Carlos.

"You should not hide from anyone son. Look, there are cars that say very little on the outside, yet have an excellent machinery relative to other cars that are more glamorous on the outside. You know, these cars are pure plastic!"

"Not only does this happen with cars dad, if you knew how many times I have dealt with people who say one thing but turn around and do another. There are a lot of fake people who do not like others just for being different," added Carlos, sitting on the couch hugging her sister who rested her head on the shoulder of his brother.

"That happens at work too. However, one must be authentic to yourself and everyone."

"We all have some talent that makes us unique, that is what my mother told me when I was young," said Araceli, "singing and dancing are two of the things I like to do, isn't it Kim?"

"Yes, mom. I like that, too!" said the girl raising her arms and waving her arms as if she was dancing.

"I like baseball and that is what I enjoy doing while going to school." Chris said.

"So it is! and you have a good arm son," Robert said, pointing and smiling.

"And the music, do not forget the music," said Carlos, raising his arms trying to catch the attention of everyone.

"Indeed, I remember now that we have a black sheep in the family," said his father, and everyone started laughing.

Carlos looked at his clock, which marked 2:20 pm. He excused himself and went to his room to get ready. He showered, changed, and went to the Help Center.

...

The car moved with difficulty through the streets of Los Angeles, which is common as there is always a lot of traffic. Rick was reaching his target, and was a few meters away. He looked at the G.P.S. following the address given to him by Ying.

The traffic light turned green and the car turned down a dead-end street. He passed a car, and without turning back, stopped near the end of the block. Fortunately, no vehicle was blocking his view and could see the driver of a car go down into a building that looked like a storage room. Rick parked and walked into the building with extreme caution. He could see that there were cameras outside the building, but the door was closed. Rick did not consider this a good idea to pick the lock, because he did not know who or what might be found inside. On the left side of the building, there was a padlocked gate overlooking a courtyard with several recycled trash cans, and saw a rusty staircase leading to the rooftop. At least from there, he could see if there was any way to enter the building. He decided to go there by climbing over the fence slightly hitting the chains that were wrapped around the door preventing entrance. He jumped and fell on the grass, which supported the fall, then wiped his hands that got dirty from the landing, looking for a way to enter the building.

Several times, he thought of the madness in which he was getting into by chasing Rex, but got a gut feeling something very bad was in there. By going through the trash bins he found a small metal crowbar just in case he needed to use it. As he climbed, he peeled paint from the metal ladder that was attached to his hands. When reaching the roof, he found it locked with a rusty padlock down into the building door. It was not too difficult to pry it open with the bar. The lock gave in easily. The building looked abandoned and was located in an area where it went unnoticed. Rick took his cell phone and put it on silent. He thought for a moment how careless he had been not having it off before entering the property.

As he approached to open the door, he heard something that left him motionless. There were screams that came from inside. He slowly opened the door and entered. He zig-zagged down a stairway to an abandoned corridor. The echo of screams was amplified and could hear that there were two people screaming. He walked down the hall which had some side doors ajar and others closed. Dirty carpet underneath amortized footsteps, and yet Rick moved as if the floor was full of broken glass. The end led him to a stairway leading down into two simple turns, under the first one he saw that the hallway downstairs was illuminated. He retraced his steps, because the screams were more intense and heartbreaking. He took out his cell thinking about calling the police, but something made him stop. It was the terror he felt when he felt the footsteps of someone walking in the lower hall. He saw a shadow, he stopped and looked for something in his pocket, and immediately directed his hands to his face, as he was putting a few drops in his eyes. Waited a few seconds, without knowing whether to retrace his steps and make a call to the police or move on. The screams were cries for help, and now again appeared to come from a person.

In an instant, several things crossed his head, arguing with Rex, attitudes held during the meeting when told the news feed, and above all, the look with an air of superiority and evil. The voice of his secretary overhearing about talking to someone saying that *"the homeless people are ready"* made him think about sending a message to Ying but decided he should go ahead to get some evidence first.

Then he prepared the camera on his phone making sure that there was nobody in the hall. Moving forward, he found an open door and saw that the room was equipped with a stretcher, some laboratory equipment, and blackboard drawings of human heads on them which different signals and frequency waves were applied. In some cases, there were red lines that clearly did not cause positive effects. Other drawings affected neural areas destructively. The most striking thing was that the table had

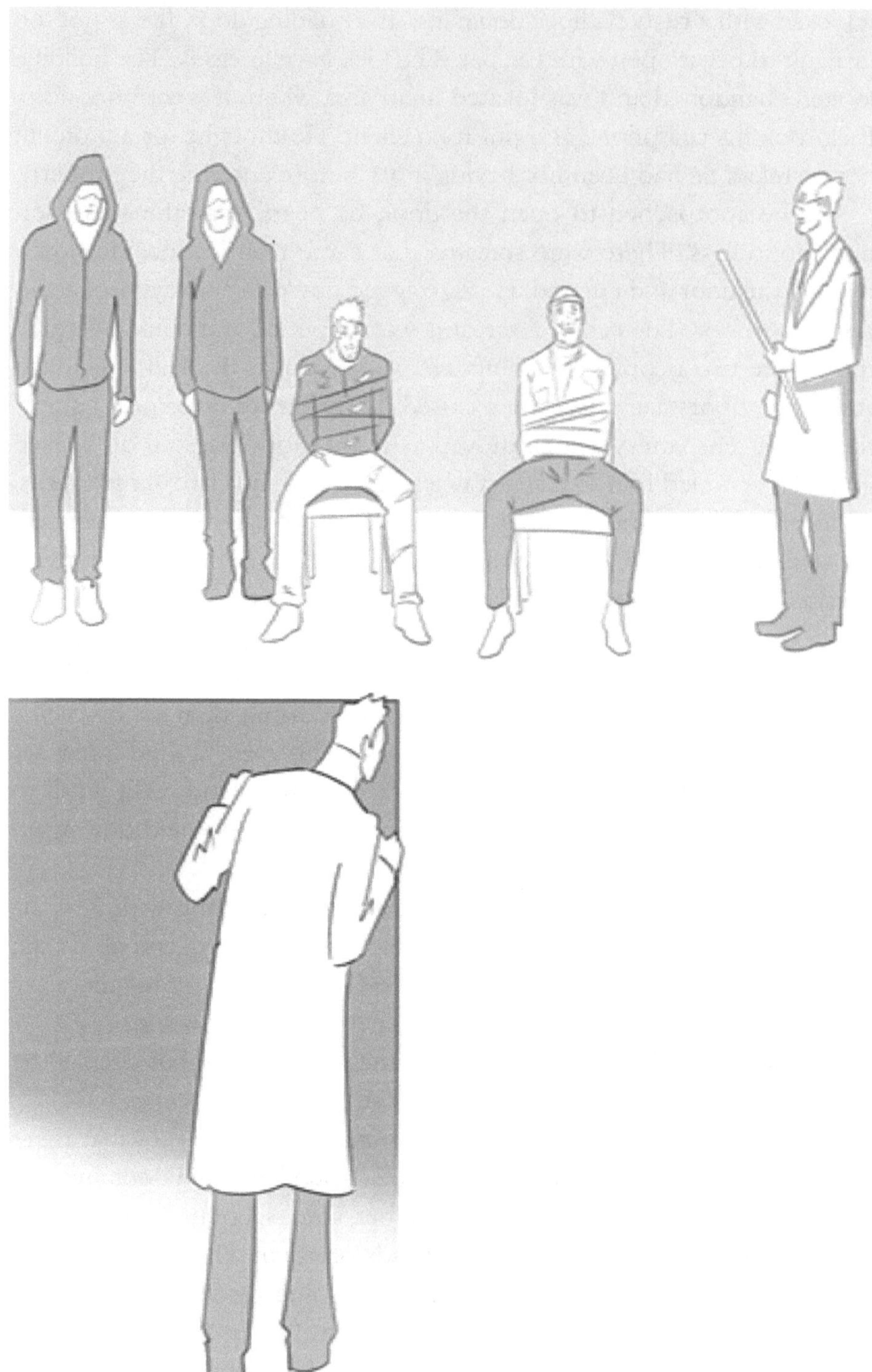

red stains but were not from an ink marker on the board.

He left the room and heard more screams, so he continued and this time it was people screaming. He turned around to the corridor and went through a door ajar. It was a very large room. There, sat two homeless men, one of them no longer looked like a human being except for his screams of pain. The other was crying and pleading, trying to move his arms and legs to remove the leather straps that held them.

Rex was standing in front of one of them with two sticks that emit a kind of shock, bringing it closer to the head, he was shaking as if receiving electroshock. He moved back when the other homeless man continued, shouting and gestured to someone Rick could not see, until he saw a man dressed in black approach and inject something he could not distinguish what was injected. The silence reigned again. Rex asked to untie the man he was experimenting on. What used to be a man, was now a disfigured animal. Rex put a type of headset on the victim, and the body began to move, too close to his hands, clawing, and tearing the straps that were loosened. After a few seconds, the homeless person rose as Rex advanced slowly and inert. Rex carried something that appeared as a stick and began to hum and then, the homeless individual began screaming and grabbed his head, and dropped down to his knees. Rick could see that the man's eyes were bleeding, as if they had exploded. His hands tugged around his hair, and tried to pull off something inside his head.

Then, Rex cursed, and ordered his henchman to shoot him. The scene happened so fast. A clean headshot blew up the homeless person's head. At that time, the other man woke up from electric shock and started screaming after seeing the scene of the body on the floor still shaking.

Rick could not move his legs, he felt they were loose and turned back his steps slowly and accidentally hit his cell phone against the wall and went back to the stairs without turning back.

In the room, Rex raised his right forefinger as if indicating to check something and motioned to the other man to investigate what had happened. Before closing the door, he could see Rex standing facing the other indigent preparing to continue the experiments.

Rick walked up the stairs very fast, trying not to make too much noise. Slid down the hallway and when he was going up to the terrace, he heard footsteps coming up the stairs quickly.

Adrenaline kicked in and he opened the door which squeaked from the light rust. Upon leaving, he saw the chain was still there with the broken lock, without hesitation went under the rusty ladder to the side of the property caught his sleeve of his shirt, which torn the button off his shirt. When he was down, he heard someone open the metal door and shook it. Evidently, they had discovered that it had not been opened due to the climate. Without hesitation, more by intuition than anything else, Rick hid by the side of one of the bins which was covered by grass. Seconds after, a figure looked down from the ceiling and went inside.

After a few seconds, Rick slipped away toward the gate and jumped back cushioning the fall with his hands. He ran to his car without looking back when his phone started ringing. It was Rex. While his phone was ringing, he opened the door and entered while searching for the keys to start the car. The phone was still ringing, and Rick was too shocked to respond. He threw the phone on the passenger seat and drove off to the office. After a few blocks, the phone rang again, and Rick answered. The voice was muffled, as if he knew it was he who had been snooping around where he should not. Perhaps too much pressure and some paranoia began to cloud the mind of Rick.

"Rex, hi. Sorry I could not answer you a while back I was in the lab calibrating the headphones, and left the phone in the office," while the other side was quiet.

"I assume you have prepared the suit before you left, your secretary said you were out."

"Yes, something came up and had to leave."

"Maybe I'm a little paranoid, but something strange has happened at the place where I am ..." said leaving a silence "...had an unexpected ... visit."

Rick felt a chill down his spine.

"A visit? Rex, I don't know where you are."

"I think you know more than you should know Rick."

"If you explain to me maybe I could understand what you mean."

"You know, I was curious to know if your clothes were torn, because we found a button with your initials."

"Go to hell!" said Rick and immediately ended the call.

The car accelerated as it headed to the laboratory.

...

The music started playing on his headphones. It was something special to him because it was carrying him to the time he met her. It was the same song that was playing in the restaurant years ago when he saw Cindy for the first time.

The theme had a strong romantic composition and every single time he heard it, his heart beats feel the need to be close to her again.

It was one of those songs that did not give you a chance not to be motived. Each drum hit with the force of the bass was like the beating of his heart. The voice and lyrics complemented the composition.

His mind connected every memory, like postcards from the time he was with her. He could see her smile, her eyes, the way she is, her charisma, her joy was all he needed in life, and represented the most important reason to go on with all his projects.

In a few minutes he got to his destination and got off the bus to walk accelerating his pace when he received a message saying, "This time I win, I am here already."

He quickly climbed the stairs feeling his heart beat fast, as if were coming out of his chest. Inside, he found Mrs. Grace and Cindy who were enjoying some chocolate cookies.

"Good day to the most beautiful women!" he said to Grace first, and then hugged Cindy.

"The heartthrob has come, see that boy is very courteous!" Grace said moving her arms wide as she approached Carlos to greet him. Cindy looked at the funny scene as she crossed eyes with the young man.

"I have prepared some cookies, help yourself son," Grace said, as she turned and took the tray from the oven.

"Thank you very much Grace." Carlos said, taking one and moving to where Cindy was.

He gave her a hug and a kiss fleetingly. He was breathing hard like a swimmer who just came out of the water after holding his breath. He asked her about Rod and the new member. In the dining room some families were having lunch, others were playing with the children who ran in search of cookies.

"I was looking for Rod, he mentioned that there is a new member at the Center."

"Oh yeah! Mr. Frank Jackson is a very polite man and friendly but very quiet," said the woman nodding her head affirmatively as she spoke and said, "Rod is on the second floor. Tell him I've saved some cookies for him too."

"Ok, I'll tell him, thank you!" Carlos said as Cindy followed.

"How long do you have until you arrive?" he asked her.

"Enough time for Grace to show me some tips on how to prepare the brownies" responded Cindy.

"And when can we eat some?" asked Carlos, in a curious voice.

"I'll take some to school. I think it would be good for you to pick me up before they are gone."

"You're blackmailing me?" Carlos said, stopping in front of Cindy, "or perhaps you have a fan?" he said, as he approached her with a shrewd face.

"I have a fan, it's a rock star," she told him centimeters from his face as she slightly bit her lip.

Carlos grabbed her waist and kissed her. At that moment it was as if his favorite song sounded and nothing else existed. However, something throbbed in his chest and then looked down with some regret.

"What's going on?" asked Cindy.

"Maybe it was not a good idea to come to talk to this man today. We could be enjoying a walk along the beach. We returned at night to the stage and I have been carrying enough stress. Being with you makes me feel good. I feel our favorite song resonating in my ears. Today before I came over I listened to it thinking of you."

She looked at him, smiled and kissed him again.

"Whatever you do will be fine. Memories of John are circling in your head, perhaps in today's presentation."

"Perhaps that is why I have to see him, that my mind does not question or create fantasies," said Carlos in a very confused manner.

"Then do it," responded Cindy.

They walked down the corridor on the second floor, and entered the recreation room. The sound of the fans inside was like being next to the sea. Inside were some people sitting down chatting, some elders walked slowly from one end to the other, stopping occasionally to look at the windows through which the reflections of the spring afternoon lit up the room.

They saw a few meters away Rodney sitting at a table next to a blind man who was playing cards. The deck was special, and each card had marks indicating what card it was.

"I got it now! This is my game. Two aces on my hands," Rod said while turning his cards relaxed, the blind man stood before him said, "I remember that movie I saw as a child that talked about a casino, although the case, it is not a casino, but a straight … really straight …" he said, turning the perfectly straight cards in ascending order.

"Oh no, is it serious?" Rodney said exclaiming in disbelief as he saw the cards on the table.

At that point, he turned and saw the couple. Took advantage of the situation to get up to greet them as the other man sat gathering cards.

"Thank God you came… I am getting plucked like a chicken at this table!" he said winking, "He is Frank Jackson and came this week to the Center."

"Nice to meet you," said the blind man, "…and you are?"

"Cindy," said the young woman, stretching her hand to greet him.

"Carlos, my pleasure Frank," said the young man, shaking his hand. The man replied with a good grip, which surprised Carlos by his force despite being in recovery. The young man noticed he made a gesture as if he had recognized his voice.

"This is the couple I told you about. They are very attentive and very loved by all residents. They brought on Friday the donations we distributed today," said Rodney.

"I feel you two make a good couple. I can feel the glow," Frank said, turning his head to the right.

"Sit down, I'll go see Grace. Before getting here she promised to keep some baked cookies for me," Rodney said, stroking his mustache.

"Grace gave us a message to tell you to stop by to get some cookies. Although you must hurry because the children are making them disappear," said Cindy smiling.

"Those piranhas …they'll see!" mockingly he said, "well, I'll be back" and immediately he left for the dining room.

Carlos looked at the man who manipulated the cards with great skill and asked:

"Rod told us that you arrived this week."

"Yes, I did," responded Frank.

"Good lesson you gave to old Rod," said Carlos in a joking manner.

"It's part of the game. There was a time when I played a lot," Frank said, with his head lost in some distant point of his thoughts, "but bad decisions led me to my ruin."

"You mean gambling?" asked Carlos, with a puzzled face.

"Yes. It was stronger than me and I lost my family, my house, my business ..." he said, staying silent.

"I'm sorry," Carlos said as Cindy who was leaning on his shoulder performing a grimace of understanding by braking the lips.

"I am too, and from that moment everything fell apart," said Frank, as though he was opening a wound.

"Your family could not help you?" Cindy asked.

"They tried to do it several times, but I only complicated things more and more. Until one day, I began mortgaging the house to pay my debts, and was the beginning of the end."

"Where there is life there's hope," Cindy said, trying to change the course of the conversation, "Grace said you were very quiet, but I see that you like to talk."

"Last week I left the hospital. The early days were not easy. It may be a signal to close my unfinished stories.

"What happened? Why were you in the hospital?" Carlos asked curiously.

"I was kidnapped," Frank said, at the table while his hands were sweeping the cards on the table, "and not only that, they also killed my dog."

When he heard that, Carlos felt like he received a slap and the barking, the muffled cry of the animal, the dog on the ground. It all came to his mind the dream images where in the end appeared John. Cindy noticed the shock and was about to ask if he was okay when young man articulated:

"God, that's awful!"

"Yes, last winter when I was returning back with my cart and Tod, my four-legged companion. I was carrying a mattress that had been thrown out on the streets. I thought that night we would sleep more comfortable. Tod was a perfect blanket for cold evenings," the man smiled sadly as he recalled the scene, "and that's when the van appeared. Two men dressed in black, with hoods got out and tried to grab me. I thought they were those guys who tend to annoy people of color. Who could care about a guy like me? But I was wrong, these guys were worse. One of them kicked Tod and that's when I took a golf club that I used to take in the cart, and I hit one of them squarely in the knee. I watched as he fell to the ground and when the other was going to hit me, Tod jumped up and bit his arm. While they were struggling, someone came out of the van and, with a gun in hand, pointed at my dog. I cried, and begged, but in a second he took his life. Then I fell down and noticed that the eyes of the men were white, as if they had no iris," he said ducking his head. "I hit my face to the floor after getting hit on the head and I saw my Tod writhed groaning, shaking his legs. I wanted to stand up, but my vision was blurred because I was bleeding. They grabbed me by the shoulders and took me to the van. The last thing I remember I was struggling with my arms and legs. I do not remember what happened, only that I was in a dark place and they placed a few drops in my eyes. That's when I went blind." Frank's face looked grimm, as he recalled what happened to him. "I do not know how many days later I woke up in the hospital, full of tubes and unable to walk. Doctors said that my head had lost brain matter by the blows. It was a miracle I was alive. I was found lying in an alley. They thought I was dead."

"Dear Lord, how horrible," Cindy said, very sensitized by the story. Carlos without missing word in his head connected pieces like a puzzle.

"I believe that fate gave me another chance. To amend my mistakes, to retrieve something from my past. I have a daughter who was very young when I lost everything. That was one of the reasons why I think I was able to get out of intensive thera ..." and before finishing the sentence, his eyes filled with tears and silence.

"Life gives us a second chance Frank. We'll help you find your daughter. You were very brave and really it is a miracle you're alive," Carlos said, looking at the man who was a little livelier with words.

"Thank you. I hope so. I see that Rodney was right in saying that you are a special couple."

Cindy took the card deck and told them both,"Mine is not the game, but I think I have a way to surprise you." He began to shuffle the cards. Frank was told to choose one.

"Ok Frank, remember that card if you want to show it to Carlos." Frank passed the card to Carlos who gave it a quick look.

"Well, now we will put it back in the deck."

Cindy created 3 rows of cards and told Frank to pick a row, underscoring columns by marking them. He repeated the process 3 times, and then all the cards were put together.

"I think I know already ..." she said starting to throw cards on the table and when all were there she removed a scattered card and said, "It's the 5 of diamonds!"

Frank smiled and totally surprised, just like Carlos wondering where she learned that trick?

Thereupon the men applauded celebrating the magic girl at the precise moment that Rodney arrived with some cookies in a basket and a thermo of coffee.

...

The emergency door opened, leaving the man a free passage to enter quickly. Entry permits had been revoked for Rick, which is why he needed the help of Ying to enter hidden in her car. Along the way, he had managed to tell his secretary what happened, omitting the gruesome details. Trying to maintain control, the discovery had left him destroyed. A puppet, a toy who had succumbed to the hidden interests of someone who had given him something to believe in. Everything collapsed once again, to the point that he saw his ideals diluted in a horizon of disappointment.

They entered his office and quickly reviewed the file transfer. Rick took the drives and backups and gave them to Ying.

"I can only trust you. I need you to keep these until everything is resolved."

"We must go now," whispered Ying.

"No, you must go now. I must do something before I go," Rick said, as he watched Ying's eyes and handed her the units and backups.

"I need to finish doing something else. I will meet you downstairs."

The woman left keeping the units in her purse, while he turned around and walked to a white desk from where he worked on his computer. Afterwards, he pulled a suitcase.

He left the office evading security cameras, while Ying descended into the parking lot in a calm manner. He went down the left wing just before another guard came down the hall toward his office.

Rick went quickly under the stairs to the fire escape exit where the doors opened from the inside without swiping the security card. Security was slow that day, however, by having his permits revoked he knew it was not going to be easy. The suitcase was not heavy yet had to take care of it with his life. When he came out the door he almost crashed into her. Upon arriving at the parking lot, he sneaked back into Ying's car after placing the suitcase in the trunk.

The car started moving and managed to leave the building. When they came to where his car was, Rick took the suitcase and went to Ying.

"I'll take my car and leave it in the parking lot and then I'll think about what to do next."

"You can come to my house, I am somehow part of this," the woman said.

"That's what I want to avoid. I do not want them to suspect you. I will go to a motel and from there I will contact you. Everything is spinning out of control and I need to think straight."

"You must go to the police. They can solve everything."

"Yes, but before I go I need to put this in a safe place and plan," he said, showing her the briefcase. "Thank you, without you I don't know what I would have done."

Ying sighed and everything seemed to stop at that time. Rick approached her and gave her a quick kiss as she closed her eyes.

The evening showed the last sun rays having their silhouettes on the horizon, as if they were brushstrokes. The farewell was quick. Before getting into his car, he saw her eyes shine, as if they had many things that should be said and even vertigo of events had thwarted against their feelings. Both cars pulled in opposite directions.

Along the way, he went to a music store where he bought an item. Several memories of his youth came to him but could not sink into nostalgia at the time. Rick left the car in a parking lot taking out what he had bought. Upon leaving, he called for a taxi to make a brief visit home.

The idea of going through the door of his house was a little far-fetched if someone saw him in his car. But he needed to get something. He also needed to talk to Ying, but he must first get his ideas organized.

He needed to calm down and talk to the police. Explain about the place of torture and the plans Rex revealed whatever they were.

The taxi turned the corner of his house, and Rick saw in front of it a parked vehicle. It could not be right at the entrance of his house by mistake, however, when passing in front he saw that there was a man by the door, and the lights were on denoting someone else was inside his place.

"Please go around the corner," Rick said, as the driver looked in the rearview mirror without much interest.

The driver asked after reaching the corner where they were going. Rick saw a man from inside his place looking at the car as if something had caught his attention. He told the driver:

"Continue please, a few more blocks down this street, I will tell in a bit the destination I need you to take."

"OK, friend. Whatever you say," said the driver moving the shifter as he drove away.

Rick understood that there was no turning back and felt everything was more complicated. He thought of going to Ying's department, but there was no way he was going to put her at risk.

"Are you a musician? Because of what you carry," asked the driver trying to break the silence as if it was a forced conversation.

"Ehhh…something like that," Rick said, taken by surprise at the concern of man. "When I was young I used to play in a band. Now, I only have memories," Rick continued.

"I have met all kinds of musicians, and they all say music is forever, it cannot be left in oblivion. It is in your blood."

"Music is always present. Even the sounds of everyday life have its own sound."

"In the city alone I hear noises, my friend. So, there is nothing better than a good radio station to turn to for making the day better," added while the volume rose slightly on radio and Rick nodded from the back seat.

"*Not everyone can hear the sound of life*," Rick thought to himself while the car was moving toward his destination.

The motel was a few blocks from a freeway entrance. That was a good place to stay and accommodate his ideas. Rick paid for the taxi and headed toward the entrance. The afternoon began to fall and still had something important to do.

He rented a room and paid in advance for a few days. Rick wanted to be alone to think and think calmly. Upon entering the room he locked it and went to the bathroom. Looking in the mirror, his face was emaciated and misaligned. He wet his face, while his head roared past images of the tortured indigents, Ying getting exposed, his son and all that the project meant for him, Rex and the organization for which he worked for, recalling meetings and details which have gone unnoticed. It was all part of a complex web in which he felt like a trapped insect. He wanted to mourn, cry, tear his heart out and even confront Rex. He knew that things were really complicated. He had to think before acting unconsciously.

At that time, a message came to his phone, but this time it was not Rex or Ying. There was a message from Cindy belonging to a message thread inviting everyone to see EZ Door in concert. There was still an ace up his sleeve and was ready to use it.

VI. SHOW MUST GO ON

There were only six hours left for the show. Carlos felt his muscles were sore after an intense morning of capoeira. That day he discovered in practice a new skill he learned, the sense of perception. When listening to music, it was like being part of it, vibrating to the beat of the environment. His mind traveled faster than the bus he was riding on. Cindy had been at the Center helping Grace and other women with dinner for Saturday night. He was planning on picking her up after band practice.

Chatting with Frank had left him some concerns that immediately related to what happened to John. Something was happening in the city which is going unnoticed. Indigents were the focus of attacks and kidnappings. For what purpose?

He thought about the bullying his younger brother suffered, all the injustices that were happening which nobody noticed.

Why humans could not live in harmony? How many souls were left as waste on the streets every year. While some looked for assistance at the Help Center, there were many others who were unprotected on the streets, especially the elderly and children who sometimes could not aspire for a future. Carlos was aware of how people looked after their own interests and there were few who were committed with such solidarity initiatives.

He was convinced that the dream that featured John was not usual, it had too much detail to be just a nightmare. Maybe it was not a good time to think about that now, he should concentrate on the concert, the show, and Cindy.

He looked up at the sky as the clouds moved slowly, as if they were veils flowing in the sky. John had taught him that trick, "... *when you feel your head is cloudy, look up. If you stare at the floor, you are at a dead end ...*" He used this trick to change his mood, especially in the most difficult moments.

When he came to Roy's home, he saw that the boys were cleaning the van.

"Hey guys, why are you cleaning the van?" asked Carlos.

"Hey! How are you Carlos? It seems that Roy wants to take his new girl and doesn't want her to know his dark side," said Ethan.

"The dark side of Roy, lol," said Carlos, slamming his hand with the drummer who returned a smile.

"There is only my light side brothers ..." Roy said, after greeting him, "get ready and I'll join you in a bit."

Carlos entered the garage where they had mounted the rehearsal room and approached his guitar. After tuning the strings began to run new arpeggios. Ethan hit his bass guitar and began to follow Carlos with the rhythm to give it more strength.

"Wow, that's new?" Roy said, entering with a bottle while Carlos nodded his head.

Roy stood behind his instruments and began to keep pace. Carlos closed his eyes. The music invaded his body completely while producing one of those magical moments in which each member seemed to be connected with the same melody. The rhythm grew increasingly stronger and the song took force. Ethan and Carlos looked at each other as if each captured the tones in which they should play. Roy swung blows, as if they were ocean waves and arpeggios soon became riffs.

The guitar was sounding melodic until the main riff and rhythmic vibration mixed with the last beats of the cymbals as the music faded. The three stars stared at each other for a few seconds.

"That was really good! I think we have a new hit," Roy said, as he searched for one of the bottles.

"And I have written the lyrics, I want to transmit something more than music with this song," Carlos said, as he took a drink.

Both Ethan and Roy were aware that the composition came from

Carlos, though he never spoke to them as if he was the owner of the songs, and always included them as part of the composition because he believed that the songs were made between all of them and that band was a homogeneous alliance where everyone contributed to the music. Bass arrangements, drum stands, choruses—all part of the process. Without them, the songs would not have the same magic.

"It's amazing! Let's create the setlist so that we can repeat it" Ethan said, hitting his bottle with Carlos and then with Roy who then looked at Carlos waiting for his order to count.

"OK let's go! 1, 2, 3 …" said the guitarist when Roy started to rip the first song on the setlist.

The setlist was tight, neat and clinching the band more in the bonds of friendship they had all along. It all sounded balanced, hard, and that was what they had prepared for that night.

After the rehearsal, they cleaned their instruments and tuned them again before placing them in the van. When all were seated, they gathered on the porch to talk.

"Just a couple of hours to shine again," Ethan said, leaning against the van.

Carlos opened three bottles and gave them to his friends.

"For John," he said raising the bottle in the air. The other two followed his lead.

"For John," they said in unison and collided their drinks.

They were silent. The drummer seemed to be staring at the floor, Ethan looked at his bottle and drank it in one gulp.

"He is with us tonight. He has never left us," Carlos said firmly.

"This new theme can be called 'brotherhood', what do you think?" Ethan said, looking at Carlos seeking his approval.

"It is an excellent name, so be it. You know, the lyrics talks about that among other things, but it sums up the bond between us," Carlos commented, "the band will not be the same if it were not so."

"The band has not been the same without John at the beginning. I think this is a very good tribute," said Roy doing a melancholic pause, then added, "we leave in ten, we still have to go to your house," he said looking at Carlos.

"And then the girls," Ethan added, smiling.

"Perfect, I will send a message to Cindy so that she is ready," Carlos said, finishing his drink.

Everything was ready for the big night.

. . .

Parking was ample and there were a few parked cars. Ying got out of the car and went to the trunk to get a bag. From the first floor, she spotted a man who was flagging her down. She went to the motel's stairs quickly. Once she reached the upper floor, he helped her with her belongings.

"With this you can go unnoticed a couple of days," Ying said to Rick, as he opened the door of the room.

"Thank you. Your help is very valuable at this time."

"You're risking your life, it's the least I can do," she said, as she came inside the room.

The woman opened the bag and pulled out a pair of pants and a black shirt that matched a black jacket with boots, socks and underwear.

"Wow, I did not know I would be a member of a rock band," Rick said, to her looking surprised at the clothing that was very different from his more conservative style.

"Nobody will look for you dressed like that. In fact, it makes you look younger. You camouflage quite well with people," she said, as she winked, "perhaps you would need to dye your hair."

"That is where I draw the line," he said, touching his hair and inviting her to sit, "I need to explain something very important about the information you have. I made a decision and to be able to notify the authorities I need to know what will happen this week in the laboratory. You will be my eyes and ears."

"Rex called asking me if you had contacted me. I said I tried to call you several times, but you did not answer me, which was usual."

"Oh, damn it," said Rick, standing up and looking out the window, "I have put you at risk again, maybe you have been followed."

"Rest assured, I have taken my precautions," she said, trying to reassure him, "I have a rental car as you indicated."

"Anyway, there is no turning back. I just hope this ends well."

"What will you do next?" asked Ying, while grabbing a notebook.

"I've already decided," Rick said, as she passed a notebook with information.

"Thank you," he said, as he looked into a folder and opened a file.

"This folder contains valuable project information. They are all technical specifications and the result of the tests we've done. The most important thing is that there is a module from which you can send and route information. While we used to make different test, it is a supplement in case any problems arise, and have to do some kind of 'Remote Play'."

"Like a co-pilot?" she asked, as she understood his idea.

"Exactly!

"It seems very complex," said Ying, while scratching her head.

"It is. You're the one to use in an emergency when activated."

"Can Rex track you down?"

"No, because it uses a new protocol transmission, which is encrypted. It will take thousands of years to discover the network and decode the signal, thus discovering its origin. Moreover, if you were on the move changing location every twenty minutes makes you completely invisible."

"Like a guardian angel," she said, in circumspect tone.

"You are. You've always been," said Rick, while smiling. She lowered her gaze shyly and continued.

"Tonight I got to do something very important. After that, I'll move again until everything is resolved. Maybe disappear for some time until I communicate with you again. So, I need you to be my eyes and ears this time."

"How will I know if you're okay?"

"Rest assured that you will know. I'm exposing you too much with this. I cannot let anything happen to you."

"Can we meet in a certain place at a certain time, periodically," she said.

"Yes, we will find a way to get in touch," said Rick, trying to be calm and realize Ying's distress, "I'll get ready since I still have something more to do."

"You need to rest, you are exhausted. You said it yourself that you need to get organized. I'll stay here if you need me to," the woman said, with bright eyes.

"I appreciate it and want it to be so. This is much bigger than I thought, and the danger is real. I have seen a person get killed."

"And you do not have to be next," screamed Ying worrying.

"I should divide my puzzle pieces, so that it won't fall into the wrong hands."

"We must seek help, maybe go to the police and the media."

He felt his heart beat go faster. His feelings were mixed and did not want to stray too far despite the risk.

"Ok, we'll do this, I need you to find me a place to stay. Then, you come here and wait for me. At this point I do not know if Rex suspects something from you and going home could be dangerous until this is resolved."

"I like that idea," she said, intercepting his gaze.

"I'm going to take a shower," said Rick, as he headed to the bathroom.

Ying turned on the TV, while Rick turned on the shower faucet. The water was slightly warm, like a summer rain renewed his energies for the night ahead.

...

The room lights dimmed, and spotlights danced on stage curtains. In the background *"If You Are Gone"* was playing while the audience shouted for the show to start.

On the other side of the stage, Carlos, Ethan, and Roy embraced each other, while saying a prayer for his friend.

"This is thanks to you brother, we know you're here with us, and we will bring the house down, just as you wanted us to," Carlos said.

It was silent for a few seconds, until one of the stage workers started a countdown of thirty seconds.

They took their instruments and were placing them in their positions. Carlos looked to the side of the stage where Cindy was with the camera. He motioned to Cindy, pointing to his ear on the song that was playing. That song was so special for them. The look between them was magical as if everything had stopped for that moment.

The music stopped, Carlos closed his eyes, and started the first chord, as the curtains were opening. The screams of the audience were amazing, the bass began to set the pace as the voice of Carlos took possession of the stage. The drums marked the hype which created the climate that was needed to set off in a burst of light. The public was frantic, singing the songs of the band, Carlos pressed guitar frets without forcing too much not to sound out of tune. The musicians moved around the stage, while the drums created a solid base that gave them energy in every note.

Music themes continued, as a succession of hits on a night that was perfect. In the middle of the show, Carlos addressed the audience:

"We thank you all for being here. It is an honor for us to play for you."

The audience cheered and applauses fell like waves before he could say any words.

"Also, tonight is very special to us, and we want to dedicate this show, and this particular moment to a very important person. John, this is for you."

The song began with an arpeggio, the lights dimmed and danced on stage, reaching a moment when the audience began to chant the lyrics. The musicians looked, felt their hair bristled, a frisson of excitement and adrenaline exceeded them. The audience hummed melodic parts and some lighters and cell phones could be seen parading on the heads as they moved side to side, as if the breeze was moving them.

After the song, the guitar remained vibrating in L.A. to the applause and cheers of the crowd, until Roy hit the plates and the bass marked the beginning of a new song.

Everything was happening at such a rapid rate that when they realized they were playing the last song. Carlos looked at Cindy, who took pictures from the VIP lounge. They crossed smiles, she sent him kisses as he winked. He was happy to be there, and to have her by his side, living a night that would last all his life on the album of the best memories.

Ethan jumped, then Roy stood up and had stopped behind the drums to a beat, while the audience chanted the name *"OEEEE OEEEE OEEEE ... E... Z ... DOOR."*

The last chord marked the end of the concert, the spotlight danced in a show of lights and lasers all over the stage and the place.

Friends gathered in the middle of the stage, Carlos lifting his guitar, Ethan left his bass guitar, and Roy stood in the middle. The three embraced each other and bowed to greet the audience as the curtain began to close slowly. Roy threw his drumsticks, while Carlos mimicked him with his pick.

Even with the closed curtain, the audience was cheering and screaming. Cindy moved quickly to her boyfriend, and both met in the middle of the stage with a kiss.

It had been a success.

"I took some videos and some pictures! You were great!" she told him, while hugging him.

Carlos hugged her back and whispered in her ear how much he loved her.

They began to put away their instruments. It was one of the few times that everything went so perfect. Going down to the dressing room, Carlos had a memory when John always came out to help them, or to advise them on how to improve next time.

He missed his friend to celebrate a time like this where the band had one of the greatest moments of success.

Cindy was with him and helped carry the bag where the drum pedals were placed, while Roy helped with the drum plates and carrying his guitar.

Upon arriving backstage, Carlos saw a man approaching wearing a shirt and black pants. The jacket gave him the air of being an old-school rocker. At first glance, Carlos could not associate with the image of the face, but he recognized certain features. Cindy was the one who screamed recognizing him.

"Rick! How is it going!" she said, and Carlos's mouth dropped wide open in surprise.

"Very good show guys," he said, as he stretched his hand.

"What a surprise! A makeover? It looks great on you!" Carlos responded.

"I must admit that reminds me of my old days, I could not come see you wearing a suit," Rick said.

"You're so cool," Carlos said as Rick greeted the rest of the band.

Cindy introduced Rick to the band, whom they thought he was a rep from a record label. Rick approached Carlos.

"Look, maybe this is not the right time or place, but I need to talk to you." The young man looked at his face, curious to know what was happening.

"Yes. No problem. Has something happened?"

"I will be brief because I do not have much time, I will be leaving for a while and I need to entrust something very important to you. Sorry that everything is planned last minute. I'll send you the address of a place where I am staying momentarily. Can you drop by in one hour?"

"I have to bring things home and get the car to take Cindy home first. I could be there first thing in the morning."

"It has to be today. I know this is crazy, but I cannot wait much longer. If it was not important I would not be asking this."

"Of course, it must be important... Dr. Rick," Carlos started to look worried, "tell me ... Rick. Where do I ...?" and before he could finish the sentence, Rick sent a message with the address of where he was staying.

"You have no idea how much I appreciate this, forgive me that everything had to go this way, but you're the only person I could trust. I have to leave now."

"Ok, I'll be there. See you in a bit," Carlos said to Rick, as he turned around and left in a hurry waving at Cindy who was watching them from the side.

When Rick left, Carlos told Cindy what just happened. Something was not right, and his mind began to go round and round. He did not know what was happening and, to make things worse, his plans were changing to a cyclical speed.

"Roy, I need you to do me a favor my friend," Carlos asked.

"Your teacher is a rocker!" he said, joking and changing his face when he saw the face of his friend, "...What happened brother?"

"I need you to take me home. I need to take dad's car. I can't go out tonight to celebrate with you guys," while Roy nodded his head, "Listen, I need something else, please take Cindy home."

"It's ok you got it. It must be something serious for you to change everything so suddenly."

"Hopefully, not so serious and I hope it's just my imagination."

"Calm down my friend. Let's load the instruments and leave."

They got things in the van. The exit was chaotic by fans, the photos, the girls who kept advancing. Roy and Ethan seeing the look on Carlos' face took him by the arm excusing themselves before leaving.

On their way, Carlos was chatting with Cindy, who proposed to accompany him.

"I need to go alone, something is not right. I'll pick you up later with the car, okay?"

"I miss you already..." she said, making a sad face.

"It will only be a moment, I'm more intrigued than you, and I miss you, too already."

The van dropped off Carlos. He quickly went inside and ask his dad for the car. That motel was about twenty minutes away, so he had plenty of time.

...

She watched from the window of the motel, looking nervously at her phone, until she felt a car entering the parking lot.

A man was carrying a bag and headed for the room. His black clothes gave him a rustic and wild look. He walked the stairs and she opened the door.

"How is everything?" asked Ying.

"Well, I brought something to eat. I was able to talk to him, and he told me he will be here in a bit."

"Perfect, then we'll leave. I talked to my aunt and she told me that we can stay at her place near the beach. At least there we can regroup."

"It will be perfect. I wanted to dine with you in a different way, but the fact is that I have to be more cautious, and with every car that passes by I feel Rex is near me."

She rested her hand on his shoulder and invite him to sit down. They put bags of burgers and drinks on the table when the phone vibrated.

Rick became fearfully, and had already blocked Rex, however, he did not know what tricks were up his sleeve.

It was a message from Carlos, "I'm on my way, arriving in five minutes"

"That was quick," replied Rick surprised in a way.

"Everything will be fine, I put the suit on the place you asked me to," the woman replied.

"Well, I'll wait below," he said, as he headed for the door.

"I'll be here in a bit," Ying said.

The night was lit by the moon, a full moon that looked like a giant over the dark sky. Rick was not hungry, but being with Ying he developed an appetite, partly forgetting their danger. He got to the car and opened the trunk to accommodate a suitcase in the back seat. He placed the item that he bought at the music store in the trunk. Everything was going as planned. He closed the car and pulled out his phone to send a message to Carlos telling him he was expecting him.

He decided to get into the car to wait for his student, when he spotted about forty meters away a figure approaching him.

For a moment he thought he was being paranoid, but no, there was actually someone who was now thirty meters away.

The individual approached slowly but briskly. He was very close now and Rick could not see his face clearly. Seconds later another man came after the first one. Rick reacted instinctively thinking that perhaps he was mistaken for a car thief.

"I'm staying at this motel, I just came to see that my car had the alarm connected."

The men did not answer. Rick had the keys in his hand and did not even know what the intentions of the men. He reached into his pockets for a few dollars that were left from the fast food.

"I have spent all the cash. This is all I have I swear, I have nothing more."

"You know why we came," said one of the men. His tone was strange, like nasal sound.

Rick knew he could not turn back. He also knew not to budge so easily for fear, after all, she was in the room and he did not want anything to happen to Ying.

"Tell Rex, I'm not scared of his games! I called the police and soon his threats will end," yelled Rick.

"Rex wants to talk to you, and bring back the suit," said one of the man questioningly.

"If Rex wants to talk he better do it personally. And he will never have the suit," Rick said holding on to the suitcase that he placed on the backseat.

"You are in no position to negotiate," said one of the men, while the other man approached slowly.

Rick tried to run, but the attacker caught his arm with a speed that left him motionless. The attacker had white eyes, as the ones he saw in the torture chamber with Rex.

He tried to push him away, but only managed to have his arm bent that made him scream.

He saw Ying peeking out the window watching the scene. All is lost, thought to himself, and above all she is exposed.

"Please stay where you are Ying," Rick thought to himself.

It was at that moment when the second man took the keys. The other man took the briefcase from the backseat of the car. Rick thought that all was lost and the only thing left was to shout out to warn people at the motel.

"I am being robbed! Call the police!" Rick yelled, before receiving a blow to the stomach that knocked him to his knees.

It was at that moment that a car turned toward the parking lot illuminating the scene.

...

The road seemed endless. Questions circulating Carlos's head about the whole situation being disturbing. The day before Rick was supposed to travel and suddenly appeared at the concert, he had a look of a celebrity, and was waiting to finish playing to approach and ask him to meet at a remote motel away from his home. What could be so important that he couldn't just trust him?

In a few minutes, there were many questions to be resolved. The motel was nearby, a large complex with outdoor and indoor parking. Carlos exited the freeway and went around to the parking lot area of the motel. A fence was bordering the parking lot, just before moving forward he saw a car and two men who seemed to be arguing. As he got closer, he noticed they were actually trying to kidnap Rick. He accelerated while the second man entered Rick's car and drove off.

A woman screamed from the second floor of the motel while other residents came out to see what was happening.

Everything fell without notice for Carlos, for his sight was fixed on the car that was a few meters away. The vehicle zig-zagged a few meters, and then turned to break one of the metal bars that was used as a divider. Carlos followed them closely making his car jump through the air falling thunderously.

"Dad, I swear I'll take it to get checked," Carlos thought changing lanes and accelerating progress to avoid losing the kidnappers. He was catching up, when the car changed lanes. The road was not too busy, however, at that speed impact could be lethal. They continued until an oncoming vehicle dodged the car and the kidnappers were driving directly toward him, forcing him to swerve off the road. He slowed down and swerved back into the other lane to avoid impact with the divider. "Damn!" Carlos shouted and again made a change and accelerated. Now, he was a few meters away.

His mind was trying to relate things that seemed incongruous, however, all events occurred again in his mind. After the death of John when they wanted to kidnap the indigent, the story of Jack, the visions, Rick's ask for help *"what mess did you get into professor..."* thought Carlos, to himself.

The chase was frantic, crossing the bridge, and passing over a lake. Carlos tried calling the police, but the maneuvers prevented him from dialing the number. He just hoped that someone could see them and report it. At that time, the kidnappers zig-zagged back and in a split second the car lost control driving off a bridge landing at the edge of a lake.

"Nooo!" shouted Carlos as he pulled the car to the edge of the bridge.

He saw one of the men leave the car and behind was Rick. Both moved awkwardly by the impact. The driver was stuck on the steering wheel that had a broken windshield. The car landed at the tip on the edge of the lake.

The young man jumped over the hijacker, who noticed his white eyes, something that scared him for a moment but delivered a roundhouse kick with the momentum of the descent. The man fell forward on his face falling into the water. Rick was sore, but achieved getting out of the car crawling on the grass and trying to walk in a clumsy manner. Carlos approached him and saw that his forehead was bleeding, and he held out his hand to help him up.

"… in the car … there …" Rick said, with some difficulty.

"We have to go," Carlos said, as he tried to lift him under his shoulder.

"No ...you have to recover ...protect it with your life if necessary ...the world depends on you ..." Rick said without being able to finish.

At that moment, the man who had fallen in the water rushed to Carlos. The young man felt the perception of the attack, and fought back quickly, but notice how fast and strong the attacker was, almost inhuman. Carlos noticed of the white eyes of these individuals. Rick had managed to get up and headed for Carlos' car getting in slowly.

The kidnapper received one of the blows swinging back and sliding on the grass, rolling down a few meters. Carlos took the opportunity to go after Rick, when he saw that another car had stopped. Two more men got out and went after Rick. Carlos went up screaming and could not let anything happen to him. He could not let history repeat itself once again.

Carlos stood between Rick and the men and prepared to attack.

As Carlos looked back, he saw the man who had fallen near the lake pulled the driver of the vehicle and carried the briefcase with him. He was stunned at how fast those attackers were. The first man lounged without uttering a word, with outstretched arms. Carlos gave two blows right on the chest that made the attacker fall back. The second man, lounged at him with the same speed as the first and began to struggle, while the other tried to take him from behind his shoulders.

It was an instinctive act, taking up shoulder to one of them and applied a lock that threw him onto the other man. Carlos' mind was connected to the rhythm of the music in his head, to the teachings of his master of capoeira, connected with his breathing, which he sought a strike point, and began beating one of his opponents. Again, they turned to attack him, but this time he did two spins on them. The first impacted the head of one of the men. The second, taking advantage of the impact, supported his leg on the floor onto the stomach with his second straight leg. The men rolled out, but everything seemed endless. Rick was near his car while the fight was going on and was leaning against the hood of the vehicle.

The man in the lake had disappeared and there was no trace of the driver. He turned to fight back the fallen one, but the scene changed drastically when he saw the men not returning to attack but go after Rick. Carlos ran and grabbed one of the men from behind him giving a blow from behind the knees to slow him down. The man fell with one leg resting on the floor, never uttering a cry. This time Carlos was not fast enough, and the other man gave him a blow to his chest that threw him back. It was as if he was hit by a car, or if he had hit a wall at full speed.

With his chest in pain, he felt short of breath as he got up. The man who fell into the lake was struggling with Rick, who could not offer much resistance, and ended up being knocked down on the ground. Now, there were two men who held the doctor.

Carlos felt helpless, angry, as if nothing could be done to defend Rick.

He heard his screams, as he was dragged to another car. In front of him, stood one of the attackers with his arms at his sides and a blank stare. He appeared to pull a gun out of his pocket. Carlos was confused and stunned for a few seconds, in which he did not know how to react, and before the attacker could pull the trigger Carlos ran toward him. Turning to aim and shoot, Carlos did the same by applying a half twist with a kick that impacted squarely on the outstretched arm and chest of the attacker. The gun fired into the ground without hurting the young man. However, because of the blows, Carlos had a cut on his eyebrow and nose. It was difficult to breathe once the blood began to spurt out.

The sound of the shot was a trigger that brought a direct memory of the death of John. Carlos moved screaming to his attacker lounging with his head into the man's stomach, and gave him two blows to the face that left him lying on the ground.

The effort was huge, with his aching fists and bloody face Carlos walked toward the car, where they had taken Rick, his muscles in extreme pain, his legs seemed about to break. He saw the doctor being dragged screaming to defend the briefcase, but a blow knocked him unconscious.

His sense of perception was put on alert, however not fast enough when he was hit in the back and fell followed later by a blow to the face.

The view got clouded by the blood that was falling from his forehead.

His vision saw a pair of boots a few centimeters from his face and watched as one of the attackers was taking the briefcase to the car and continued on their way.

Carlos could not sit up; his muscles were so sore that he only managed to turn to his back.

The car departed and he was quietly watching the stars shine, as they were the only witnesses of what happened, until the brightness was lost and he passed out on the road.

EPILOGUE

The night was dark, the streetlight lit up like a projector falling vertically. Everything was so unreal that it had to be a dream. It was not real, it was not a reality. The last thing he remembered was that he had to meet with Rick, the persecution, the white-eyed men.

"The suitcase," was the first thing Carlos thought when he came to.

He turned around, but there was nobody. He wanted to move but was still sore. He could not move, just watch. Everything moved as if there was an earthquake.

Everything was bright. There was still darkness from the night that left some darkness and the light of the streetlights lit up his face. The dry blood was glued to his eyes, made them hard to open. The phone was vibrating and managed to wake him but he could not answer it. All his bruised body ached, it felt hard to move. He rose gradually, the best he could. His head exploded in pain. He wanted to have superpowers to deal with the situation and fly or recover quickly, but his whole body was bruised, dried blood and pain.

It took about fifteen minutes to reach the car that had fallen on the side of the lake. The two front wheels were impacted in the mud. The driver's window was broken and there were no occupants. He found the car keys and looked inside to see if there was something that could give him a clue of what has happened and where Rick was taken, but he found nothing. But then he decided to open the trunk.

Inside there were only emergency tools and a guitar case. He found it very odd to find a guitar case there. He accommodated it on top of the trunk. He noticed it was not too heavy despite the size of it.

He leaned on the trunk door, coughed and opened the locks disengaging the case. Inside was an envelope that read *"M-Clave,"* on one side and the other said, *"the future of this world is in your hands,"* and had a bag inside.

When he opened the bag, his eyes widened in surprise and smiled as the adrenaline began to run down his body once again.